AMY REDEK

Homos Ubique

GROUP SHARING EROTICA

WARNING

This book contains sexually explicit scenes and adult language. It may be considered offensive to some readers. This book is for sale to adults ONLY.

Please store your files wisely where they cannot be accessed by underage readers.

About the Publisher

4Fun Publishing, a member of **BLVNP Incorporated,** 340 S. Lemon #6200, Walnut CA 91789, info@blvnp.com / legal@blvnp.com
NOTE: Due to the highly emotional reaction of some people to works of erotic fiction, any email sent to the above address that contains foul language or religious references is automatically deleted by our anti-spam software and will not be seen. All other communications are welcome.

DISCLAIMER

Please don't be stupid and kill yourself. This book is a work of FICTION. Do not try any new sexual practice that you find in this book. It is fiction and not to be confused with reality. Neither the author nor the publisher or its associates assume any responsibility for any loss, injury, death or legal consequences resulting from acting on the contents in this book. Every character in this book is over 18 years of age. The author's opinions are not to be construed as the opinions of the publisher. The material in this book is for entertainment purposes ONLY. Enjoy.

Homos Ubique
Group Sharing Erotica

By: Amy Redek

ISBN: 978-1-62761-871-7

Chapter One

When I was courting and finally married Cyndi, I didn't know that she was bi-sexual. In fact it was two years after our marriage that I found out by accident. That was because I arrived home earlier than normal as we'd had a problem at work and they closed down early, the reason's not relevant, but what I found at home was.

I'd parked the car in the garage and went in via the back door which wasn't locked and expected to find Cyndi in the lounge, but was wrong, and wondered where she was. I knew she was in the house because of the back door not being locked, and so I assumed she was in the bathroom. Wrong again, for she was in the bedroom. That was then a shock for me, for she was not alone, for there was Vera on the bed with her. What was more, was that both of them were naked and Cyndi was between the legs of Vera sucking and licking at her pussy.

I was transfixed at the sight, never having dreamt that Cyndi was bi-sexual, plating another woman. I hadn't made any sound opening the door so they were unaware that I was there, hearing the sounds of Cyndi's sucking and the moans being given out by Vera, squirming about at the ministrations that she was getting, her eyes closed and her hands pounding the bed as I guessed by her movements that she was just about to have an orgasm.

I saw her body writhe on the bed and then relax at having had her release before she opened her eyes.

'Christ!' she exclaimed, her legs closing against Cyndi's head, making her squirm and bring her hands up to prise the legs open for her to breathe and speak.

'What the hell you doing?' Cyndi asked, looking up at the wide eyes of Vera.

'It's him!' she cried, her face now a bright red in having been caught in the act. 'Your husband!' pointing at me in the doorway.

'Oh shit!' Cyndi said, turning her head for me to see her eyes wide open as well now, her face going red and saw that her lips and mouth were wet from the juices of Vera. 'What are you doing coming home so early?' she asked, moving out from between Vera's legs that closed up and her rolling over onto her stomach, burying her face into the pillow.

'More to the point,' I said, looking at her naked body as she turned and sat up, 'is what the hell do you think you were doing?'

'Having sex, you prat! What else did it look like?' was her retort.

'Why?' I asked and then realised that it was a stupid question.

'Don't tell him,' came the muffled voice of Vera from the pillow.

'Why not?' Cyndi replied, half turning her body and giving the cute bum cheeks a stroke before turning back to me. 'It's because we like it. We've been having sex together ever since school.'

'But you're now married....to me!' I cried.

'So? I like having sex with you as I also like having sex with Vera,' she replied.

'But two women doing it together. It's.....it's not right,' I exclaimed.

'Men do it together as well as women,' she came back at me. 'Maybe you should do it and then everything would be alright. Why not try Bruce? He's gay and I'm sure he liked to have it with you.'

Bruce was a friend of ours, both of us having known him for years and quite often came round to our house for a drink and a chat. So with her saying that he was gay was news to me for I hadn't guessed, even though he was single. Little did I know what was running through her mind at this point but I found out a few days later.

'Now get out of here and let Vera get dressed,' she said, getting up from the foot of the bed and pushing me out of the bedroom. With her then closing the door, I went downstairs and poured myself out a drink, musing over what she had said about Bruce. The number of times we'd been together was uncountable and I hadn't picked up on the fact that he was gay in all the years I had known him. What was more was that I hadn't twigged that my Cyndi was bi-sexual either. I heard the front door open and close a minute later and guessed that it was Vera leaving and Cyndi came into the lounge and got herself a drink and sat down wanting to know why I was home so early. I told her and then went on to mundane things without Vera being mentioned again.

***

IT WAS a few days later that Bruce called round, me not knowing that Cyndi had invited him. It was early evening when he rang the doorbell and I answered it.

'Hi, John,' was his greeting, holding up a six pack of beer.

'Hello, Bruce. Come in, anyone with beer is welcome,' I said and he entered and went straight on into the lounge with me following him.

'Hello, Cyndi,' he said, moving over and giving her a kiss on the cheek. 'I haven't come empty handed.'

'I can see that,' she said, taking the cans of beer from his hand and putting them on the coffee table and pulling the wrapper off, got a can out and popped it open. 'Just what the doctor ordered,' she said after taking a mouthful. Both Bruce and myself popped a can each and drank some as we sat down. 'How about a D.V.D.,' she said getting up and moving over to the television set and selected one from beneath the set and inserted into the player and turned both on before sitting back down.

It was a porn movie that she'd put on and it was of two men meeting in a room, kissing before stripping off and showing that they both had an erect cock as they kissed again, stroking each other's erection. She had turned down the sound as we saw one man go down onto his knees to start sucking on the other man's erect cock, taking quite a bit of the length into his mouth. Quite a few close-up shots of the head sliding in and out of the open mouth and getting tongued at the same time.

'That's what I like to see,' Cyndi said. 'Two men sucking on each other. Why don't you suck on Bruce,' she asked, looking at me.

'What?' I replied, shocked at having her make that suggestion.

'I said, have a suck on Bruce's cock. You'd like him to suck your cock, wouldn't you, Bruce?' she asked, looking at him. His face had lit up at her suggestion and gave his lips a lick with his tongue.

'Yes, I would. I'll even suck on yours too, John,' he said with a big smile. 'You'll enjoy it. Tell you what. I'll suck on you first, okay?'

I looked at them both, a bewildered expression on my face at the suggestion, but felt my cock starting to make itself felt at the thought of being sucked upon by another male.

'Come on, the pair of you,' Cyndi began. 'Get those clothes off and let me see it for real instead of on the television. You've seen me suck on a pussy,' she said to me, 'now let me see you suck on a cock.'

There wasn't any change to the expression on Bruce's face so he must have known that Cyndi was bi-sexual and following her words, had stood up and was then taking his clothes off. It wasn't until he was fully naked with his erection jutting out from his groin did I suddenly realise that maybe it wouldn't be such a bad thing to do and slowly began to take off my clothes. I revealed that I too had an erection and noted that we were both of about the same size in the cock stakes.

I'm sure my face was red at doing this, standing naked in our lounge facing another naked man while my wife looked on.

'I'll start the ball rolling,' Bruce said, moving over towards me. 'Sit down and I'll suck on you first.' I amazed myself by sitting down, my cock still standing out in front of me, now wanting him to suck on me and....and then sucking on his cock that was now in front of me.

He knelt down onto the carpet and shuffled forward in between my open legs and rested his elbows on my knees and took hold of the shaft of my cock and gave it a squeeze. It was throbbing away and the foreskin was stretched halfway down the bulging head that had taken on a purplish colour and had a thrill run through me at having another man, for the first time, holding my erect dick in his hand. I saw him lick his lips first as he smiled up at me lying back in the chair before he lowered his head and took half the length of my erection into his mouth.

God, his mouth was hot as he engulfed the head, pushing the foreskin right back with his lips as he did so. Then to have his tongue move over and around the bare flesh made me quiver with delight it was so erotic. My body had been tense at first but now I relaxed and leaned back and closed my eyes but not before seeing Cyndi watching this act with eyes wide and a smile on her face. She said something but with the euphoric feeling I was getting by having my cock sucked, didn't catch what she was saying.

How nice it was to have Bruce not only move his head up and down on the head of my cock but have his hand moving on the shaft in an opposite movement. It was exquisite and so good that I knew I was not far off from cumming in his mouth and wondered if he was going to swallow it or not. Cyndi had only sucked on me once and when I did cum in her mouth, she spat it out. But that thought soon passed from my mind as I gave myself up to the thrill of feeling my sperm rise up my cock and erupt into Bruce's hot mouth. He didn't stop his sucking as I came, not once, but five times I spurted out my seed and felt an extra suck as I think he then swallowed what I had given him for he never lifted his head up from me until my prick had started to soften.

The air felt cold round the head of my cock when he lifted his head up and smiled up at me before bending down once to again to plant a kiss on the head before leaning back onto his heels.

'That looked good,' Cyndi said and I nodded at this for I had enjoyed it.

'It tasted good too,' said Bruce, his eyes shining. 'I can't wait for it to rise up again for some more.'

'Your turn now, John,' said Cyndi, and this made me start to tremble, never having done this before. Bruce got up from the floor, his erect cock swaying at his movement, my eyes not leaving the sight of what I would shortly be having in my mouth, and in front of my wife too!

I slowly heaved myself up from the chair and moved to one side for Bruce to then sit down with his legs apart and his cock appearing to be straining his foreskin fit to burst. It was if I was in a dream as I felt and saw myself moving forward and going down onto my knees between his legs and leant my elbows onto his knees as he had done with me. His cock now looked huge with it just in front of me and with a trembling hand, took hold of it and unconsciously licked my lips as I looked at the fiery head, having a deep red colour to it. I closed my eyes and bent my head down and took the head of his cock into my mouth.

It felt very hot as my lips closed round the bare flesh, the foreskin having moved down with my mouth movement, and I could not only feel his cock throbbing in my hand, but in my mouth too. Bruce gave out a groan as I began to use my tongue as he had done to me and I sucked on my first cock and had a surge of elation that I was giving him some pleasure in what I was doing.

A thrill ran through me at what I was doing, sucking on another man's cock and felt that I was enjoying it. It was like having a hard and yet pliable lump of rubber in my mouth as I gently chewed on the head as I sucked, my hand firmly moving the soft skin of his shaft up and down over the solid bar of flesh that it covered.

'I'm going to cum,' I heard Bruce say, and I held him more tightly as I moved my hand on him and I actually felt the head of his cock swell a little more as his hips bucked up slightly as the first surge of his semen came erupting into my mouth. It hit the roof and back and nearly made me choke as he cummed and cummed until I thought that I would never be able to take it all.

I felt his body relax under me when he'd finished cumming and I wasn't sure what to do now with the head of his cock still in my mouth, covered with his cum and the only thing to do was swallow it as he had done to mine. This I did and felt the whole mass of it slide down my throat and felt my own cock start to rise again at what I had just done and felt on top of the world at having this new experience. One that I was never going to forget, for I found that I just loved having his throbbing cock there and having just swallowed his cum.

I ran my tongue round the head, cleaning up the last remains of his cum, getting the slight taste of it before finally releasing him and giving the head a kiss before sitting back on my heels to see him smiling down at me.

'For a first timer, that was very good, John,' he said to me.

'Yes,' Cyndi added. 'It looked good, was it?'

'I don't know what to say,' I stammered. 'But, yes, it was,' feeling my face redden at having had her see me sucking on another man's cock. 'It, er, well, er, it wasn't as bad as I thought it would be.'

'Well, that's the answer your cock is saying,' Bruce said looking at my erect piece sticking up from my groin, 'it looks as if it wants to be sucked again.'

I looked down to see that I was indeed up and hard, the foreskin halfway down the red fleshed head and it now began to throb at the suggestion and I looked up at Bruce with, I think, a silly grin of my face as I then nodded my head.

'Well stretch out on the carpet and I'll blow you again,' he said. I didn't quite get the connection that having a cock sucked was known as a blow job which appears to mean the complete opposite. I did as he asked and moved and lay full length on the floor as he got up from the chair and lay down beside me, though he lay in an opposite position to the way I was lying. My erection was up, laying on my stomach which he lifted upright with his hand and began to move his hand up and down and I got a thrill again at having the soft skin moved over the hard flesh beneath it. He leaned over and blew into the eye that opened to his squeezing and I could see a bubble of clear fluid at the tip.

'Ah, love juice,' he said and licked it off with his tongue and rolled his eyes as he looked at me. 'Beautiful. Lovely and sweet.' He went on to say that some people called it pre-cum, but he preferred to call it love juice. 'Sweet as honey and if this could be produced in quantity, you could make a fortune it's so delicious. Now roll onto your side so that I can suck you properly.' This I did with him already in that position, holding my cock in his hand and I know found my face just opposite his flaccid penis.

I gave out a groan as I once again had the head of my cock taken into his hot mouth and had his tongue roving over the bare flesh he had revealed with his pushing down of the foreskin. I saw his limp dick give a twitch and I now wanted it back in my mouth too, so I leaned forward and found I was able to take the whole limp piece of flesh into my mouth and have my nose up into his pubic hair. His dick, I was calling it that now with it being soft and when it became hard and stiff, then it was a cock. But it was now just like a soft piece of rubber that I could bend about in my mouth with my tongue, which wasn't for long as I gently chewed on it with my teeth and tongue.

I was almost swooning with the pleasure I was getting as he used his teeth to rake the bare flesh of my cock head as well as his sucking of it and I then had his dick start to harden up and it was soon pushing up into my throat making me move my head back a little as it grew in my mouth and became a cock. I began to copy him in the way he used his teeth and tongue to excite me, especially when his tongue stroked its way over the G string. That small piece of skin that was attached to the foreskin at the base of the head and he told me later that this was just one of erogenous zones of the male body.

It was also exciting when he released my cock from his mouth so that it flopped onto my stomach and he could then nibble his way down the underside and make my whole body quiver and I shuddered completely when I felt him take my balls into his mouth to roll them round in their sac as he sucked at the same time. It was only for a moment or two before he released them and nibbled his way back up my cock and took the head back into the warmth of his mouth. I was nearing my peak now and he didn't need telling as he felt my body begin to stiffen as I started to jerk my hips towards him and stopped myself just in time at clenching my teeth down over his cock head as I came in his mouth, sending a big shot of cum into it as he also worked it up the inside with his hand movements.

His cock was now really throbbing in my mouth as I came in his and could see his leg muscle move and knew that he was about to come too and I was ready and had the first burst of his cum hit the back of my throat, almost making me gag again, but it was okay as more was pumped in, feeling it coming up the tube that was on the underside of his cock and when I stopped shooting my load, his was still coming into my mouth, filling it once again and I had a shiver of pleasure run through me at being able to taste his cum again.

I copied him in rolling it round in my mouth, coating that still throbbing cock before taking a deep breath and sucking as hard as I could and to have it all slide down my throat. We licked each other clean before finally releasing the head to feel the waft of cool air move over the exposed flesh before flopping onto our backs. I was over the moon at having had this experience and was now glad that Cyndi had almost forced me into having this form of male sex. Little did I know that this was just the beginning of turning me into a bi-sexual man who would then be craving to have sex, in all its form, with other men.

***

BRUCE HAD gone home but not before giving Cyndi a kiss and a deeper one to me, his mouth open for his tongue to be able to push against my lips to open and have his tongue inside my mouth. Christ! I got another hard on at feeling his tongue move and caress mine in what is known as a French kiss. He had finally moved away from me with a smile on his face and gave the front on my trousers a stroke.

'I can't wait for another invite,' he said, looking at me first before looking at Cyndi.

I was tempted to say that he should come round the next evening, but Cyndi got in first by saying that it wouldn't be long for she had enjoyed seeing us two suck on each other. I had enjoyed it better than I thought I would have, but kept quiet as Cyndi might have taken my comment the wrong way.

With Bruce leaving, Cyndi and I went up to our bedroom where she started to get undressed, revealing her perfect body that gave me another erection which she saw when my trousers came off.

'Are you thinking of me or Bruce?' she asked as she lay back on the bed with a smile on her face.

'You, darling,' I lied, even though the sight of her open legs and the inviting view of what she had there was enough to raise a dead man.

'Well, you've sucked on Bruce, now suck on me,' she said as her fingers were already caressing her clit. Obediently as ever, I gave her a smile back and climbed on the lower end of the bed and moved my body up, squashing my erection as I moved in between her legs and started to use my tongue on the inside of her naked sex.

It wasn't long before I had her thighs trying to squash my head, her body starting to squirm and she soon tugged at my ears.

'Now, John, now! Put it in and fuck me!' she cried out. In spite of the urgency of her voice, it still took me time to prise her legs apart to let me move out from my licking of her to move up and let my cock slide up and inside where my tongue had just been working. Boy, she was hot and I had her internal muscles flexing themselves around my cock and shaft as I buried it as deep as I could inside that oven as it seemed to me then.

I hadn't even got myself up onto my elbows as her legs came up my sides and had her heels digging into my kidneys as her fingers dug deep into my shoulders as she started to buck herself upwards, really fucking herself on my rampant cock before I'd even started to move myself.

In fact, I didn't have to move at all because she was doing all the bucking as though she was trying to dislodge me.

'Yes, yes, yes,' she cried out as all her muscles seemed to be trying to squeeze the life out of me as her body went rigid and I felt that hot gush of her orgasm start to slide round my hard cock and even start to coat my balls. I came too, sending my cum up to try and fight the down flow of her as my seed was moving upwards.

I was still cumming inside her as she suddenly relaxed and went limp beneath me, her legs falling away from my sides like a deflated blow up doll and I'm not sure she even noticed that I had cummed inside her.

'Wow, John! That sure was one hell of a fuck,' she said, her eyes shining. 'I think it was because of the sight of seeing you and Bruce sucking each other that made it the best yet.'

I had no answer to this as I had now just finished in cumming inside her and was striving to get more air into my lungs before I pulled out of that body heated interior of her pussy. I gave a groan as I did so and rolled over onto my back and had her rise up to move down and take the head of my cock into her mouth to suck off both the coating of her juices and suck out any remaining traces of my sperm.

'We must have Bruce around soon if this is what we can have afterwards,' she said after letting go of my prick that was now subsiding. 'In fact, instead of it just being you two getting your rocks off, we'll make it a threesome so that I can have a bit of the fun.'

There was nothing I could say to this, and so she took my silence to be an agreement before we went off to sleep.

Chapter Two

It was a couple of evenings later that Bruce came round again. I didn't know that Cyndi had phoned him. I opened the door to see him standing there with two six packs in his arms and a smile on his face and I'm sure that he saw my eyes light up.

'Hello, John,' he said as I stood aside to let him enter and as I pushed the door closed, he moved into me and gave me a light kiss on the lips. I was surprised but not shocked at this kiss and glad that he had the beers held to his chest so that our bodies didn't touch for he would have certainly felt that almost instant erection I had got at seeing him in the doorway.

'H...hello, Bruce,' I stammered, loving the look in his eyes and licked my lips at the kiss he had given me. 'Nice to see you again so soon.'

'And seeing you too,' he said. 'I was thrilled when Cyndi rang me asking me to come round. She said that the other night was so erotic for her that she would like to join in and make it a threesome.'

Well this was news to me and wondered exactly what she had meant by it being a threesome. Did she want to suck on his cock too? Or was it to let him fuck her with me watching? My mind went into a whirl at this thought and wondered if I could handle that, having her being fucked by another man in front of me. There was only one way of stopping that and it was for me to get in first. I somehow thought that just me sucking on him again wouldn't be enough and wondered if I dare go so far as to having him fuck me instead.

Now that was a thought for I hadn't had a man put his cock up my ass and tried to visualise me actually going that far in sex with another man. Alright, I'd sucked him the other night, the first time in doing this and now would I go so far in having him fuck me? I pondered on this as I led him through to the lounge where he put the beers down as Cyndi moved into his arms for a kiss.

'Hello, Bruce. Glad you could come,' she said with a smile.

'Well I'm here but I haven't cum yet,' he replied, them both then laughing at the pun he made. She turned and ripped open a six pack and handed both Bruce and myself a can that we popped open to take a gulp of beer.

'Shall we go up to the bedroom?' she asked, 'and take another beer with us?'

Bruce and I picked up another can as she had done and we followed her out of the sitting room and up the stairs. I had butterflies in my stomach as I followed Bruce, watching his bum move from side to side as he went up the stairs. Would he let me fuck him if I let him fuck me? I thought. I was almost drooling at the mouth I had so much saliva there at the prospect of having his cock again in my mouth, and maybe, up my ass for the first time.

Into the bedroom we went with Cyndi being the first to put down her cans and start to strip off her clothes, being naked before us and saw all that she had, especially when she climbed onto the bed. She lay on her back to watch us take our clothes off to let her see that both of us had erections that stood out proud from our groins.

'Come and join me,' she smiled, pushing the pillows onto the floor as she moved over to one side, her tits swaying nicely with the movement. 'You lie on your back in the middle,' she said to Bruce, which he did, his cock then lying up on his stomach. I was looking more at this than her as she went and straddled his head so that he was looking straight up at her pussy. 'Eat me, Bruce, as I watch John suck on you,' and lowered herself down as his hands came up to stop her actually smothering him. I could hear him start to slurp as I moved between his legs, pushing them wider apart for me to get in properly and lifted his throbbing cock upright in my hand.

The head was a dark red that was showing inside the stretched foreskin and with a squeeze of his hard cock brought out that pearly drop of love juice from the eye. Now I had already tasted mine when it came out of my cock, nice and sweet and wondered if his would taste the same. I leaned closer and used my tongue to lick this off and felt him shudder a little at my touch. It was the same, sweet and absolutely delicious taste and wished that more would come out it was that nice to take in and savour.

Now I opened my mouth and with my lips pushing his foreskin right down, took that glowing head into my mouth, loving the feel of it throbbing as I began to run my tongue round the bare flesh that felt quite hot to my tongue. I started sucking on him and then paused, the thought of having this what was in my mouth up in my ass. Could I? Should I? Can I? Well, stop sucking this cock or he'll cum there and you'll never find out what it's like, a voice said in my head.

That made me decide to have his cock in the only other place it could go and pulled my head up off of him and let his cock flop back onto his stomach as I quickly got off the bed and went and got some lube out of the bathroom. He was still eating out Cyndi who gave me a strange look, not knowing what I was going to do, but the light dawned as she saw me start to put some lube over the head of Bruce's cock. I looked up to see her smiling and I'm sure that I had a stupid grin on my face as I then shuffled by body up above that of Bruce, holding his cock upright until it was above the cheeks of my bum. With me being astride of him, I knew that the cheeks would be parted enough and slowly lowered myself down till I felt the head of his lubed cock at the entrance to my virgin ass.

Now was the moment of truth. Could I take the whole of his throbbing cock inside me or not? I took a deep breath and tried to make my inside body relax as I let my body down slowly, feeling the head of his cock start to widen my ring piece. Relax, relax, my mind was shouting out as I was getting some pain there at having my ass expanded more than it had ever been. But this was then superseded as I felt the head slip in and felt it throbbing inside me and I could hear a snort from Bruce with his head still under Cyndi's pussy as he did so.

Oh, what bliss to then let my body down even more as I felt his shaft now filling my backside, throbbing away until I came to rest, sitting on his thighs with that pulsating rod of iron giving me all sorts of new and strange, exciting feelings within me.

'Another first, then,' Cyndi said, leaning forward on her knees but keeping her pussy down over Bruce's mouth as she pulled my shoulders towards her to kiss me. 'What's it like for you, for it's certainly good for me?'

'It....it's, er, great!' I stammered, telling the truth, for it was really thrilling to feel his hard cock throbbing and pulsating away inside me, making my sphincter muscle to constantly flex itself round the shaft at the entrance. 'It's an incredible feeling,' and I began to lift myself up and down in this different mode of fucking. Which really was me doing the fucking of myself on Bruce's cock, not the other way round. I even closed my eyes as I moved up and down on him, loving the feel of his hardness sliding inside me, sending all kinds of different sensations up through my body. The main one being the pleasure I was getting of having him there and knew then that I would want it again sometime in the future.

Then came the icing on the cake. Not icing per se, but cum. I felt the head and whole shaft start to swell a little and suddenly felt the spraying of his cum as he shot his load up into my ass. I felt it coat my canal as it came out of his cock, not once, but five times I felt it hit my insides and I drooled at this added pleasure of having him cum inside me.

I could hear the groans coming from Bruce as he cummed inside me and with Cyndi's hands still holding my shoulders, felt her grip me tightly as she began to squirm over the face of Bruce and saw her whole body give out a shudder and a small scream came from her throat as she had her orgasm. There were all kinds of grunts and snuffling from Bruce as she obviously filled his mouth with her outpourings.

God, I was in heaven having his throbbing cock inside me and having him coat my channel with his cum that added to the lube and made it slide more easily there, but now I wanted his hard cock in my mouth too, so with reluctance I might add, I lifted myself up. I didn't really what to but the urge to suck on him was greater now that he'd cum inside me. I felt it slowly coming out of me as I lifted myself up and because it was now coated in his cum, didn't feel any pain as the head finally emerged from my backside.

I quickly got off the bed, my legs feeling quite rubbery as I went into the bathroom and soaked a flannel which I took back and gently washed his cock, taking the time to really clean the head and shaft. I tossed the flannel to one side and lay down and took the still hard cock head into my mouth to gently chew and suck on it. I even managed to draw out a little bit more of his sperm that had still been inside.

As I sucked on him, I saw Cyndi lift herself up off of Bruce and I could see that his face was quite red before Cyndi's hair blocked my view as she kissed his wet lips. I only had a few more sucks before Cyndi pushed my head to one side as she then took his cock head into her mouth to carry on the sucking of him. I moved up the bed until I was lying alongside Bruce.

'That was just great, man!' he said to me after turning his head towards me. He couldn't move much with Cyndi lying half on top of his legs and looking down to see her bobbing head on his cock that she had one tit being squashed between his legs. 'What did you think, being on top of my cock?' he asked.

'As you said, Bruce, great!' I grinned. 'That's the first time that I've had a cock up my ass.'

'So would you like it a second time then?' he asked, his hand now holding my erect cock in his hand and slowly moving it up and down. 'After fucking me with this lovely hard cock?'

'Too right, Bruce,' I replied grinning at him, my cock now throbbing fit to bust, 'before I cum all over your chest with what you are doing.'

'Move, Cyndi,' Bruce said, giving her head a push. 'John's now gonna fuck me.' She lifted her head up, letting his fiery cock head free to bounce up onto his stomach.

'That's going to be something to see,' she said with a smile on her face, moving to one side to let Bruce roll over and raise himself up onto his knees. I too moved at the same time, getting up onto my knees and grabbing the lube and getting some over my pulsating cock before shuffling round to get between his open legs. With his legs being wide apart, he'd opened up the cheeks of his bum and I could see the target to aim for as I put my left hand onto his hip and held my rigid cock in the other as I moved in closer until the head was touching the entrance to his backside. I felt his body flinch at the first touch and my heart glowed with this being my first time that I was just about to shove my cock into a man's ass instead of a woman's pussy.

With my cock being held in the right place by my body weight, I brought my right hand up to his other hip and slowly leaned in towards him, feeling the head of my cock being slightly compressed as I watched it start to slowly disappear into his asshole. Christ! The heat that surrounded the head when it slipped in was incredible and I felt his inside muscle start to flex itself round my shaft as that followed the head inside him. Bruce had given out a couple of grunts as I started to fill him with my cock and when I was fully inside him, my thighs tight up to the cheeks of his bum, I gave out a gasp at the lovely tingling that ran through my body at now having my throbbing erection inside another man.

'Wow! This is great, man,' I cried as I began to move myself in and out of him. Well not quite out, just bringing the head back to the entrance before pushing it back inside him. I was in another kind of heaven at the tightness of him as compared to the slackness of Cyndi's cunt. This was nearly as good a feeling compared to having his cock reaming my backside which I think was slightly better. What a joyous feeling it was to be moving my cock in that heated channel, having his muscle constantly flexing itself round the shaft as I moved.

I looked over to see Cyndi smiling as she watched me fucking Bruce, giving her lips a lick, her eyes shining at the sight of me fucking another man. But this pleasure was coming to an end as I felt my sap rising and so held his hips in a tighter grip as I started to ram myself harder up into him to his grunting, pulling him backwards onto me as I pushed harder at him, my balls swinging below and smacking up against his lower bum cheeks.

Then I erupted inside him, and what a relief it was to feel it shooting out of the eye of my cock to coat the insides of his canal, making it a smoother ride.

'Lovely,' he crooned at feeling my cum spray his insides as more came out of me and into him. Five loads he got before I came to a stop, holding him tight up to my thighs as I pumped out the last drops, then slowly leaning over his rear end and found that I was panting really hard as it seemed to have exhausted me.

'Great, man! Just great,' he said and then gave out a little cry as I began to pull out, his muscle now really clenching itself tight round my withdrawing shaft, trying to hold me back but to no avail and I slipped out to an obscene popping noise.

Cyndi, bless her, had retrieved the wet flannel from the floor and now began to wipe the head of my steaming cock, well it appeared to be steaming, before running it down the shaft that was still erect and throbbing. Bruce had fallen onto his side as I then got off the bed and went and washed my cock properly and when I returned, saw that Bruce now had another hard on and had a big smile on his face.

Seeing that it was there ready for me, I couldn't get back onto the bed quick enough, taking hold of it and putting the head into my mouth to suck and give it a coating of my saliva, knowing that I was now going to have it back up inside me again.

It didn't take long for me to be on my knees with him behind me and once again, for the second time now, had another man's erect and throbbing cock pushed up into my rear. What bliss it was after that short bit of pain as my asshole was widened to gain entry and feeling the hardness fill me with joy at having it again throb inside me.

This was actually better in this position than me bouncing up and down on it for he was doing the moving and I can't describe all the emotions that flowed throughout my body as I got the thrill again of having that hard flesh throbbing away inside me. Even more thrills came as he held my hips firmly and he began ramming hard into me and felt his cum start to spray inside me, making me drool at the pleasure I was getting by being reamed in this way. So much so that I started drooling at the mouth having it dribble down my chin. Not only that but had felt my cock rising up hard again as it was bouncing beneath me and having my balls swing back and forth.

I could hear his heavy panting as he came to a stop, his cock still throbbing away inside me and felt drops of sweat land on my back as he leaned over my rear. I too felt that I was sweating and shook my head to stop it getting in my eyes and saw that Cyndi had a big grin on her face and saw her move over onto her back and she slid underneath me as I was in this kneeling up position.

Her mouth was hot as she took the head of my cock into her mouth and began tonguing and sucking on me and didn't have to use her hand for me to start cumming in her mouth. Boy, wasn't it a lot she got! It didn't seem to end as the last drops splattered her face with me moving my body backwards. This was because Bruce had started to pull out of me and I moved back to try and keep him there, throbbing inside me. As hard as I could, I used my inside muscle to grip and try to stop that wonderful tool from leaving my backside, but lost out as the entrance to my ass was widened slightly as the head left my body. I felt like crying at it no longer being inside me.

But that's life, as pleasure is always just a fleeting moment of time, but I was now resolved to extend this pleasure as much as I could in having a cock either in my mouth or up my ass.

***

BRUCE THEN came round once a week for us to have a threesome of sex on our bed that lasted for eleven months before he moved out of the area because of a promotion where he worked. That was when Cyndi started straying. Sometimes not even coming home at night and we would have furious rows over this as she wouldn't tell me where she had been. Or more to the point, who was she having sex with when not at home for the night. Was it another woman or another man I wanted to know for I was now missing having a man suck and fuck me too.

Our arguments began getting rather acrimonious, so I made my decision and moved out and got a place to live in another town.

Chapter Three

It was easy enough to get another job that paid enough for me to rent a furnished one bed apartment in a five-storied block, my one being on the third floor that had three other apartments on the same level.

It didn't take but a few days before my next door neighbour made herself known to me. Her name was Carolyn, single but had a boy friend called William. She was quite an outspoken young woman and it didn't take long for me to learn that both she and her boyfriend were bi-sexual, a point that made my body tingle. A fact that made me tell her that I too was bi-sexual and was, at present, separated from my wife.

She must have told her boyfriend about me for it was less than a month that she invited me to go with her to her boyfriend's place which I might enjoy. This I interpreted that it would be a threesome of sex with her knowing that I was bi-sexual as they were. So with her in my car, went and stopped off for her to pick up some beers and we were soon at his flat not far from our place.

I liked the look of William at first sight when he opened the door and welcomed us in, him being about a year or two younger than me, good looking and appeared to have a good body which I shortly found out that I was right. We shook hands as we were introduced and Carolyn got a kiss as he took the beers and led us into the sitting room where three cans were popped as we sat down and talked.

The talk eventually got round to our bi-sexuality, which I think I was being summed up first before it came round to that, for it was then asked if I would like us to have a threesome of sex. It was smiles all round when I said yes and so with a beer each in hand, went into his bedroom.

William was the first to strip off to reveal that he had a nice looking cock sticking out from his strong looking body, hard and erect that I now wanted both in my mouth and up my ass. Carolyn had her clothes off before me to show that she was slim with a perfect pair of tits that befitted her size and had a nice trimmed triangle of hair between her upper thighs. By the time I got my clothes off, I had an erection that sprang into view when my shorts came off.

'Damn! It's bigger than mine,' William said, sitting down on the bed looking down at his standing up erect cock.

'You should enjoy sucking on it then,' Carolyn said as she got onto the bed behind him, moving her hands round his chest to stroke his nipples. William nodded his head and beckoned me forward, which I did, moving in between his spread legs for him to open his mouth and take the head of my cock inside.

His mouth was hot and he had pushed my foreskin down with his lips and I now had his tongue moving over the G-string, making me quiver with delight as my hands came up to gently hold his head as he sucked and pleased me with both his tonguing and sucking of me.

'The pearl was lovely and sweet,' he said on letting my free from his mouth. The pearl being the love juice that always comes out when I have an erection. 'I hope that your seed is just as good,' he grinned up at me. 'Come,' and he giggled at the word, 'and join us,' moving himself over for me to get on the bed with them.

Carolyn climbed over our bodies as I was told to lie in the middle on my back, which I did and watched as she got astride of me, showing her wet pussy which was lowered down to be just above my face. She was then looking down my body as William got between my legs, pushing mine apart as he lifted up my cock and took the head back inside as his hand began to slowly move up and down on the shaft. Carolyn then lowered her body further for me to start licking her insides and get the sweet juices from her body.

Her clit was as hard as a nut and big enough for my teeth to be able to gently scrape it, making her shudder before my tongue flicked over it in between pushing it up into the entrance of her vagina. William was giving me pleasure down below with his tongue as he sucked and also played with my balls at the same time.

With having sucked Cyndi for some years now, I was quite good at cunnilingus and soon had Carolyn trying to mash herself down on my mouth, but had learned to have my hands up by my face so that I could still breathe while tonguing and sucking on a woman's cunt.

With William bringing me to my peak, I managed to hold on till I had Carolyn give out a scream and a shudder as she had her orgasm, sending down quite an amount of her fluid, filling my mouth which triggered me off to letting me then fill William's mouth with my cum. He was like a hoover as he sucked it up and felt that extra bit of suction as he swallowed my cum as I tried to drink Carolyn's juices.

Carolyn moved up off of me and moved down the bed to push William's head off my cock so that she could get a taste as she took over. William then moved up alongside me to lean over and kiss me as well as lick the juices of Carolyn from my chin and upper lip. Our mouths opened for our tongues to play with each other as Carolyn kept on sucking on a now wilting organ. I felt William's hardness pressing up to my thigh and now wanted to suck on him and it took quite some effort to push him over and pull my cock out of Carolyn's mouth for me to slide down the bed and hold up William's hard and rampant cock.

The head was bulbous and stretched his foreskin so that it was halfway down the head, the fiery flesh a dark red colour as I felt the blood pumping round to keep the whole cock up and hard. I gave my lips a lick as I looked at it and opened my mouth and took it inside, pushing the foreskin right down to have the bare flesh throbbing in my mouth. I did the same to him in the teasing of the G-string, making his body quiver that I felt as I lay over his thigh.

What pleasure it was to once again have a man's cock back in my mouth to suck and tongue as I moved the silky skin up and down the hard flesh that it covered. He gave out a groan and felt his body start to tense up and knew that he was almost there in his cumming into my mouth.

Wow, it surged up and the first salvo hit the roof of my mouth as his hips bucked beneath me, sending up more and more to fill me with his cum that joined up into one mass that swirled round the bare flesh of the head. My heart was hammering away at feeling it fill me and was beside myself with pleasure as I then swallowed, to let it slide down my throat like an overgrown oyster. It was lovely, simply lovely to once again have the pleasure of tasting and ingesting another man's cum.

It was several more minutes before I released his cock with it starting to deflate and lay back and had a beer can pushed in my hand and loathe as I was to wash his cum out of my mouth, drank some and saw that they were drinking beer too. Carolyn then squirmed her body in between ours as we drank our beer before speaking.

'Two lovely big cocks to fuck me when they've recovered,' she grinned, 'and you can fuck me first, John,' she added as she took hold of my cock to rub it. And rub it she did, making it rise up quicker than I'd known it before, well I think it was because she'd also moved down the bed to start sucking on it too. So it wasn't that long before it was up in the fucking mode and she released me and lay back and spread her legs for the ferret to find its burrow.

She smiled up at me as I got between them and getting up onto my elbows, moved my body up ever closer till the head of my cock touched her sex, making her give out a groan. This turned into a gasp as I pushed myself right up inside that wet and slippery vagina, pushing up until our pubes met and I could get no further into the heated interior.

Her eyes that had been closed at the first touch of my cock now opened that I was now fully inside her and she smiled up at me, her vaginal muscles flexing themselves round my throbbing cock that twitched in response. I smiled back at her and glanced over at William who was smiling too and I got an extra thrill as I felt his hand start to caress the cheeks of my bum.

He kept stroking me as I began to fuck Carolyn until her legs came up by my sides, knocking his hand away from moving over my bum. Then got a shock that made me stop for a moment as his hand had then taken hold of my balls. With the gentle manipulating of them, I then carried on fucking that lovely hot hole of hers but also was thinking that it wouldn't be long, I hoped, before I could then fuck the tight hole of William. What I would have liked then would be having William fuck me at the same time as I was fucking Carolyn, but she wanted him after I had finished with her, so it was a thought that had to be put on the back burner for later, though I wondered what would it be like to be fucking another man's backside while being fucked myself. Food for thought.

But having these thoughts running through my mind brought me up quicker to my orgasm and so with big shudders on top of Carolyn, came inside her, giving her my new supply of cum, hoping at the same time that she was on the pill which on reflection, must have been, otherwise she wouldn't be letting us both fuck her without the use of a condom.

After giving her all of my current supply of sperm, came to a full stop, panting heavily before pulling out to her cry of dismay, her muscles trying to hold me back to no avail and I came out and rolled over onto my back.

'Boy! That was some fuck, John,' she panted as I saw William start to move himself in between her legs, his cock bouncing up and down making me wish that it was being pushed up into me. It was with envy that I saw his throbbing organ slowly being pushed inside Carolyn's body until it was out of sight but unlike William, I waited until her legs moved up his body before I began stroking the firm looking cheeks of his bum as he started to fuck her, batting on a sticky wicket. He too flinched like I had done when I took hold of his swinging balls as he moved inside her and held then until he started to cum, feeling them move up in their sac as his seed was being released from inside.

I watched his coated prick slide out of her and it smacked up onto his lower belly as he rolled over onto his back and I was quick to move over and take the glistening head into my mouth to suck on her juices as well as suck out any sperm left inside his still hard erect cock.

Whether she was miffed at me sucking on him first, I don't know, but she went and straddled him and lowered her sex down onto his mouth and heard him slurp away at the juices that were still coming out of her vagina.

With both of them cleaned up and William's cock head nice and shiny, we all sat propped up against the headboard of the bed and drank another can of beer each as we said how wonderful it had been for the three of us. Though I was anxious for William to rise up again for my backside was now itching for him to push his cock up inside me to scratch away that itch that was now starting to aggravate me.

As the empty cans were put to one side, Carolyn started to use both hands on our limp cocks as we lay either side of her.

'Come on! You're supposed to be men! Let's see these cocks rise up for I want to see you fuck each other,' she said, her hands moving quite fast as well as gripping them tightly, well mine she was. It was the thought of having his lovely tool inside me made mine rise up first, though he wasn't that far behind in having his up in a fucking mode.

'Fuck me first, John,' William said, 'then mine will just that bit stronger for you afterwards.' As much as I wanted him now, his suggestion was a better idea, so I moved out from Carolyn's grasp as he pulled free too and got up onto his knees, spreading his legs for to move in between them. It was a sight to see, his bum cheeks slightly apart for me to see the puckered hole that I was going to shove my prick into. Which I did, holding his hips firm as I rammed myself straight up inside to his gasp at my rough entry into him.

'Christ! It feels bigger than it looks,' he croaked out, his muscle now flexing itself round my shaft.

'It didn't hurt you?' I asked before I started moving myself inside him, just letting lie in him as it twitched away of its own volition.

'No,' he croaked again, 'you were in too fast for my body to react, but it feels great!' I'm sure my sperm was seething inside my balls at me not moving, waiting to be shot out, though what they didn't know that it was to their death and not having to fight to be the first to fertilise an egg cell. They were going to get their wish to shoot out as I then began to move in fucking the tight asshole of William.

How lovely and tight it was, moving my cock in that slippery channel that was his asshole, holding him firmly as I moved my cock slowly backwards and forwards, feeling his muscle keep clenching itself round the shaft as I fucked him. But with the thought that he would soon be doing the same to me made me start to cum. The cum building up to be a mass at being the first shot which was copious to say the least as it shot out from the eye of my cock in one bloody great stream. William gave out a little cry as he felt this first emission of my cum spray his inside canal, his muscle clenching itself round my cock as I pumped away sending more and more up to add themselves to the first load.

Empty. Drained and exhausted, I came to a stop, leaning over his rear end, seeing drops of sweat fall onto his lower back as I panted away, trying to get more oxygen into my system.

After breathing deeply, I slowly straightened up and began to pull out of William, hearing a muted cry from him as I did so. His muscle gripping me really hard but it wasn't strong enough to hold me there, lovely as the fuck had been, I pulled out. I moved and flopped over onto my back and had Carolyn quickly over to take my wet cock into her mouth to suck on me in spite of the fact that I had gone bare back into William.

He had slowly fallen over onto his side, his erection was really throbbing and twitching as he smiled at me.

'Boy, that was one glorious fuck, John. I only hope that I can give you the same pleasure I've just had from you,' he said, still taking in deep breaths. I looked at his throbbing cock and my heart was jumping about inside my chest, my mind crying out to have it inside me. So pushing Carolyn's head off my cock, managed to get myself up onto my knees to a big smile from William as I assumed my position in the middle of the bed.

Carolyn moved first to give his cock a suck to coat it with her saliva and with it being done, I watched him get up onto his knees and shuffle round, out of sight as he got behind and in between my open legs. His left hand was on my hip as he got in position and gave out a shiver as he stroked my bum first before letting me feel the head of his cock touch my ring piece between the open cheeks.

I relaxed as best I could but still had some pain as his head started to widen the entrance and all of a sudden, it was inside me. Glory! He was in and his shaft quickly followed and I had his throbbing cock pulsating away inside me, making me come out in goose bumps at the thrill of having his hard piece of meat where I had really wanted it. I was in heaven!

His right hand came to my other hip as he started to move himself backwards and forwards inside me, making me tingle all over at the lovely sensations that his hard prick was giving me. I even found myself drooling as he slowly shafted me, loving every move he made in giving me the greatest thrill in our form of having male sex.

He must have wanted to fuck me as much as I wanted him to, for it could only have been a matter of minutes before I felt his fingers dig deeper into my flesh as he began to pull me back onto his forward thrusting, knowing that he was about to cum inside me. Come he did, shooting his cum in with some force that I felt coating my inside channel with each and every spasm of his lovely throbbing cock. I even began crooning as every shot was felt, being added to the first load of cum. What joy it was to feel this with his cock now sliding more easily as he massaged my insides until he came to a stop, leaning over my rear as I had done to him. Hearing him panting and feeling drops of sweat land on my back, his cock still twitching away inside me.

I almost sobbed as I felt him pulling out and tried to hold him there with my muscle but failed and had my ring piece expanded a little but without any pain as it finally left my ass. It brought to mind that time is a fickle thing. Misery seems to last forever whilst joy passes in a flash. How true it is when applied to you just having been fucked.

It was an hour before either William or myself were aroused again to tackle Carolyn to start all over again. It was lovely.

***

IT WAS two weeks later before we had a threesome again, this time it was in my flat and it was as good as the first time. Fucking both Carolyn and William and having William fuck me, with Carolyn also being chewed out by the pair of us.

We got together again after another two weeks had passed, using Carolyn's flat this time where we all had the pleasure of fucking and being fucked. In fact, we did this for well over a year but there were also some changes to this pattern that didn't include Carolyn.

Twice a week, William would come round to my place and I would then go to his the following week.

'Do you mind if we're to be naked all the time I'm here alone with you?' William asked on our first one-on-one in my flat.

'Not at all,' I said, taking him into my arms for us to kiss. 'I like seeing your lovely body without clothes, especially what you have that I want all the time,' stroking his cock and bringing it up to a full erection. This made it difficult to get his lower clothing off but it was soon out in the open, bouncing about which I soon stopped by going down onto my knees and taking as much of it as I could into my mouth to suck, tongue and chew. He would then do the same to me though with us doing this at the point of undressing was only our form of foreplay for we would get a beer each and sit on the couch and watch a porn film before we really started to suck on each other till we shot our cum into each other's mouth to savour the taste before swallowing the cum.

After resting and seeing the end of the film, we would then go to bed where we would once again be in the position to take it in turns to fuck each other. How glorious it was to have his lovely big cock reaming my asshole and having him cum inside me and then giving him the same pleasure.

So it was two nights a week with us being naked, we sucked and fucked in my flat and then two nights doing the same at his and then having our threesome with Carolyn. Though this came to an end about nine months after we had started having sex in a threesome, for Carolyn landed a plum job, the drawback being that it was in another town. So our last threesome together was a period of tears in between us fucking each other as much as possible and only coming to a stop as dawn was breaking, both William and I really exhausted and completely out of juice.

We were both at her apartment on the day she left, tears and kisses were passed over as we waved her goodbye and I think it needless to say that William and I then went to bed to fuck each other. But it happened again that we would be parted for William himself had a job offer that he couldn't refuse and so we both went through the trauma of having our last suck and fuck before he too left town.

What a miserable three months I had with being on my own and only having my right hand to give me one side of having some sexual relief until out of the blue, Cyndi came back into my life.

Chapter Four

Since our breaking up and me moving to this town, she had also moved to another town and it was from there that she had found out where I was now living and begged me to join her and start all over again. She vowed that she had changed and would not stray as she had in the past that led to our parting but she still wanted me for what she realised what she had lost by her straying.

What with her crying and begging that we tried to repair our marriage and the fact that in spite of what she had done, she still was a good fuck which was what I was missing now being on my own. So I agreed, and a week later, we met up and with more tears and kisses, I moved into her flat where the first thing we did was to go to bed.

She quickly undressed, showing me that lovely body of hers, her breasts still up and firm with the nipples quite outstanding, firm and looking like hard nuts. Her pussy was hidden by the trimmed bush of public hair between her thighs and now naked, rolled on the bed and looked up at me with a smile.

'Come on, John. You don't know how much I have missed you these many months,' she said and so I took my clothes off slowly, looking at her naked there on the bed made my cock start to rise for I had been without sex for months too. I saw her lick her lips when my trousers came down to reveal my hard erect cock and I couldn't stop it twitching of its own accord. So naked, I got onto the bed and into the arms that held me for quite some time, for us to kiss and get my erection pressed tight to her side. 'You look and feel as big as I remember,' she murmured between kisses, her hands stroking my back as I lay half on top of her. 'Did you miss me?'

'Of course I did, Cyndi,' thinking of us having a threesome together with one of her lovers, wishing that one of them was here now to fuck me as I fucked her. For I was now, since Carolyn and William, into men, or rather they were in to me which I now wanted as much an erect cock as she did pushed up inside me. To feel that exquisite pain as my hole was widened to then have it smoothed away by having that rampant cock sliding back and forth inside me. But not only that, but being able to suck on one, to run my tongue over the bare flesh of the head to feel the man shiver at the touch and for him to then give me his cum for me to taste and savour before swallowing it. But I was back with Cyndi and at least she did like me fucking her and I enjoyed it too and so I moved over her lovely body and got in between her open legs.

She gave out a big sigh as I started to slide up into her pussy, feeling it rather wet with her juices that had already started to flow. It rather felt as if my cock was being sucked into her as I moved once again into that soft and hot interior until our pubes met and I could go no further. I could feel her muscles flexing themselves round my now throbbing cock as I kissed her before raising myself up onto my elbows to start moving myself inside her.

'You always were a good fucker, John,' she gasped at the first prodding I gave her, her legs coming high up by my sides and her fingers starting to dig into my shoulders. As I was ramming myself into Cyndi, my mind was wishing that I had William lying on my back with his hard cock moving inside my back passage. Having these thoughts of him fucking me as I fucked Cyndi, made me shoot my load after less than a minute inside her. I had moved up so that my arms were rigid either side of her as I rammed myself into her as I gave her my cum.

'Too soon, John, too soon,' she cried out as she felt my cum hitting her insides. 'You must have missed me by cumming so quickly.'

'That I did, Cyndi,' I lied, panting away as I finished cumming inside her and falling onto her front, squashing her lovely tits with my chest. Her arms came round my neck to squeeze me tighter to her as she kissed me before she started to push me up.

'Let me suck on that lovely cock you've got,' she said, her eyes shining, her mouth changing slightly into a moue as I started to pull out of that hot interior to then roll over onto my back, my wet and shiny cock flopping up against my stomach. 'I swear you've got bigger,' she said as she moved and held my cock upright, her hand getting smeared with our cum, and quickly bent her head and took me into her mouth. This was as hot as the other hole I had just vacated, her tongue licking off the juices and also sucking any residue of my cum out of my cock.

Looking down at her head bobbing up and down on my cock made me wish that it was another man doing this for I would have him upside down to me so that I could then be sucking on his at the same time, giving him the pleasure that I was getting by having my cock sucked. There was an itch up my backside that only another cock could scratch and gave out a groan as I flexed the muscles in my bum to try and stop this itching, making my own cock throb at the same time.

'You must like this, John,' Cyndi said, briefly letting go of me to speak. 'It's really throbbing.' She gave me a grin and took me back inside her mouth to carry on until it started to wilt somewhat.

It took an hour before I was up and rampant again, having already gone down between her legs, kissing, licking and sucking at her wet pussy and even managed to bring her to an orgasm, having her juices flow down into my mouth for me to suck and drink. She had another one when I fucked her, having her fingers rake my back as she humped herself up at me as I rammed in her cunt, shooting out my cum as she cummed too.

***

AS WE both worked, our sex was nearly every night and weekends, though with me being freelance, I was able to spend most of my time at home, doing a lot of my work through my computer. It was in some of my spare time that I cruised, if that's the right word, the internet and found a chat channel for gays. I scrolled through and didn't realise that there were that many men and women who were gay and wanted to talk to others of the same ilk. This is how I got to know Toby. I finished up talking with him for he lived in the same town as me and lived not far from where I was living.

He freely admitted that he was into men only for sex where I had to say that being a married man made me bi-sexual, and because of this, wanted to meet sometime. This I agreed to for he was only a year or two younger than me and seemed the right kind of guy that I could handle. This last word having more meaning if you know what I mean.

So we met in a bar by agreement and hit it off straight away, both of us liking the look of each other and it wasn't long before he asked me to go to his flat for a bit of fun. I was all for this as by sitting there talking to him, I had gotten a massive hard on and said we'd have to wait a little while until I would be able to walk out without showing that I was in that state. He gave the front of my trousers a stroke and smiled at me.

'Just what the doctor ordered,' he said. 'I'm having the same problem,' taking my hand and rubbing his crotch with it. It felt as big as mine and I almost drooled that within the hour, I would have it in my hand, mouth and up my ass. We had to talk of mundane things until we had both subsided till the front of our trousers looked normal before we finished our drinks and went off to his flat.

It was only a five minute walk from the bar, about the same time distance of mine but in the opposite direction. It was a one bedroom flat in a block that he lived and I was quite pleased at how clean it was inside. He beamed at me saying this and took me into his arms and kissed me. That started us both off in getting erections which could be felt as we held our bodies close in our embrace.

'God, I need what I can feel,' he said with a smile as we broke off the open mouth kiss that we'd had, having our tongues play with each other.

'Me too,' I replied. 'It's been some months since I had a man like you in this state and in my arms.'

'Well, let's see if you've not forgotten how to use it,' he said with that lovely smile of his. So he led me into his bedroom which held a double bed and he quickly pulled the top covers off before turning round to me and started to undo the buttons of my shirt. With the front open, he ran his hand over my chest, tweaking the nipples before baring them and taking one into his mouth to suck and nibble on. When he stopped, I then did the same to him, feeling his hairless chest and his nipples up hard as nuts for me to do the same in the sucking and gently chew on.

We stopped briefly to get our shirts off before he unbuckled the belt of my trousers and pulled down the zipper to be able to ease them down past my knees revealing that I was indeed hard and filling my underpants with my throbbing cock. He gave out a sigh as he smiled at me and rubbed the front before sinking down onto his knees and slowly pulling down my underpants till my cock sprang free to bounce right before his eyes. He then gave out a groan and took half of the length into his hot mouth, pushing the foreskin right back for his tongue to run over the G-string, making me give out a shiver.

'No, Toby, no,' I cried, pulling myself out of his mouth. 'You'll make me cum too soon. I'd rather we did it together on the bed.'

Which I think he wanted too for he was quickly up and getting the rest of his clothes off as I got my trousers free from my feet, getting my shoes and socks off too. I saw his cock as he stripped and saw that it was as big as mine with it being erect and almost started drooling at the sight of it bounce about as he moved. With us both naked, we got onto the bed and into a clinch to kiss and tongue each other for a few minutes before he broke off from squashing our cocks between us and moving down the bed in an upside down position to me.

So with us both in the sixty-nine position, we looked at the throbbing cock in front of us before taking the fiery head of the cock into our respective mouths. Unlike me, he had been circumcised, having the foreskin cut away but it still retained the G string which I was able to tease with my tongue when I had his cock there in my mouth.

What joy it was and a pleasure to once again have a hard rampant cock in both my hand and mouth for me to play with, in the sucking, tonguing and gently chewing of the hard flesh of another man as was being done to me at the same time. I was in heaven again as I sucked, having already taken in the pearly clear fluid of his love juice. So sweet that I wished that a cock could produce more of this honey like nectar.

It wasn't long before I felt his hand that was moving up and down on my shaft grip me tighter and moving faster, guessing that he wasn't far off from cumming. So I did the same and it wasn't long before we started to groan round the cock in our mouths that we let fly and cummed into each other in great gouts of our sperm. What a glorious feeling it is to know that you have brought this about in making this other man cum and fill the mouth for you to taste before swallowing. Moving the mass around with the tongue before taking a deep breath and letting it all slide down the throat, wishing that more would come out of the eye of the cock you are sucking.

We seemed to be copying each other in the aftermath of our cumming, squeezing the cock hard to try and bring up any residue left inside to swallow and then licking all over the fiery head to clean it up. With a final kiss we gave to each cock head, he turned round on the bed and came up and kissed me, our tongues still retaining a little taste of our cum.

'I think we both needed that,' Toby said. 'I just loved having your cock in my mouth and can't wait for it to rise up again for you to fuck me with it. My ass is already itching for it.'

'Me too,' I said with a grin on my face. 'It's been quite a while since I had a man like you fuck me and I think yours is the best yet.'

So for nearly an hour we lay together, stroking each other's body, especially of the flaccid piece of meat in between kissing until we were both sporting hard and rampant cocks again.

'Well, we're both ready,' Toby said as he broke off our cuddling to get off the bed. His cock was bouncing nicely as he did so and went off to the bathroom to get some lube, the cheeks of his bum moving nicely as he walked and I nearly started to drool at seeing what I would shortly be sticking my cock in between.

'Let's do it doggie fashion,' he said, squeezing some lube onto his fingers. 'Let me fuck you first.' Well it was his flat so I had no choice really, and I rolled over and went up onto my knees, spreading my legs for the rabbit to see its hole. My body gave out a shiver as I felt a lubed finger touch my entrance, moving round the puckered portal before being pushed inside me. I gave out a groan as I felt it moving inside me before he pushed a second one in to start to relax and widen me. He even finished up with three fingers moving inside me that made me start to beg to have his erection take their place and it was only a moment or two after them being pulled out did he start to put himself inside me.

His left hand came onto my hip at the same time as I felt the head of his cock nestle itself at the entrance to my ass and with his right hand coming onto my other hip was when he leaned forward. I felt the pressure of his cock start to widen me even further and had a little pain as it forced its way in and gave out a gasp as the head finally slipped in, feeling much bigger than it looked.

It was like a man dying of thirst being given a bucket of water having the head and shaft smoothly sliding into my inner channel, ironing out any kinks and quelling the itch that I felt inside me. I was in heaven again at feeling his cock throb away inside me, my muscle constantly flexing itself round the solid bar of flesh as it reamed me. Like a well-oiled piston, it moved back and forth, creating exquisite little tremors as he ploughed my meadow, making me tingle all over.

But the pleasure of being fucked by another man is not one that lasts very long, and he was soon gripping my hips with his fingers as he started to pull me back onto his forward movement as he began to ram himself up into me, almost lifting me up from my knees in doing so.

For what we are about to receive I muttered to myself and receive it I did. The first blast of his cumming shot deep into me, feeling it coat my canal and aided the smooth reaming I was getting as another salvo hit me to be followed up by another four of lesser degree, but what a thrill that was to actually feel his cum filling my backside as he came to a grinding halt. His thighs that had been smacking the cheeks of my bum were now pressed up tight to me, feeling his cock still throbbing away as he leaned over my lower back, panting quite heavily.

The pressure of his fingers ceased as the palms of his hands pressed down for him to straighten up his body and felt him start to pull out. At this, I groaned for I was losing what had just given me an enormous thrill as well as a now enormous cock that was throbbing away, but with the thought in mind that it would soon be up his backside in a few minutes.

I gave out a little cry as the head slipped out for me to feel the cool air waft round my shrinking asshole as he then got off the bed to go to the bathroom to wash himself having just fucked me bare back. I slowly eased myself down onto my front being careful not to squash my throbbing cock too much, reliving those last few minutes of having such a lovely cock ream me and next felt a wet cloth being used to wipe away any excess lube from my ring piece. What a thoughtful man in doing this and got another surprise as he then gave each cheek a kiss before getting back onto the bed. I rolled over and sat up and gave him a big kiss for the pleasure he had given me and then moved over to find the lube as he got into position for my turn to fuck him.

With him on his knees and his legs spread wide, I was able to see his rosebud that I was going to fuck and lubed my fingers first and stuck one up inside him, making him flinch at the first touch. That finger slid in easily and so I pushed another one in and then a third to find that he was relaxed okay and so put some lube on the head of my cock and got in between his open legs.

I shuffled forward, holding his hip with one hand and my throbbing erection in the other as I placed it at the entrance to his ass. I felt him give a little flinch at this first contact and teased him a little by moving it up and down over the rosebud, causing him to call out.

'For fuck's sake, John! Don't tease me! Put it in and fuck me, will ya!' his voice full of exasperation.

So with it firmly held at the entrance by my body weight, I held both hips as I looked down and watched the head of my cock being slowly compressed a little as it started to disappear into his ring.

'Oooh,' he crooned as the head widened him and then, 'Aaaah,' as the head disappeared inside to be followed by my shaft till my thighs were tight up to the cheeks of his bum. 'That's lovely,' he panted as his muscle began flexing itself round the shaft of my cock, making it twitch in response in that hot interior of his backside. 'It's big, it's throbbing and it feels fucking great! Now fuck me!'

This I did, loving the tightness of his asshole as compared to the slackness of a vagina and the internal body heat as well as the flexing sphincter muscle, stronger than those inside a woman. What bliss to be holding the hips of a man as your cock slides beautifully backwards and forwards in that lovely canal, hearing him croon as he's being fucked up the ass, then to hear the words most often used.

'Fuck me harder, John. Harder! Let me feel your balls smacking my bum.'

So I gripped Toby's hips tighter as I moved into ramming speed, pulling his hips back as I moved harder into him, feeling my balls bouncing between the cheeks of his bum, almost lifting him up from the bed such was the force being used. But by ramming myself up into him so hard, my swinging balls agitated the sperm inside and I was soon holding his rear end tight to my thighs as I began pumping out my cum up into his ass.

He cried out at feeling the first salvo hit his insides which was repeated as more followed, coating his channel with my cum until he had all I had to give in this session and leaned over his back as I came to a stop.

'Lovely, John,' he crooned, my cock still throbbing away, beating a tattoo to his insides. 'It's given me a hard on. Stay inside and jerk me off.' I now heard that he was panting the same as I was as I reached down beneath him and found his hard cock, throbbing and pulsating away as mine was. It was hot and hard and I gripped it hard and began moving that silky skin over the hard solid flesh inside. 'Yes, yes,' he panted. 'I'm nearly there already.....I'm....cumming, I'm cumming......aaaaaah,' he sighed as I felt his cock swell that little bit more and felt his cum moving up the tube to shoot out of the eye of his cock. Five shots he had in his cumming, the last being more of a dribble that I felt running down onto my fingers, and when I released him, this I licked off and looked forward to when I could have another mouthful to get that lovely taste of his cum again.

He gave out a cry when I pulled out of his rear end, knowing exactly how he felt at losing what had just given him pleasure. But now being out of the body heat, the air felt cold round my prick as I got off the bed to go to the bathroom to wash myself.

On returning to the bedroom, my now slowly deflating cock swinging between my legs, I saw that he was lying on his back, his semi hard cock now lying limp across one thigh as he smiled at me. He opened his arms and I got onto the bed and into them, half lying on him as I went into the embrace for us to kiss each other.

'That was just great, John. I've been needing a cock such as yours inside me for quite some time now,' he said after we'd broken off the kissing and lay in his arms.

'That it was, Toby, for I needed it too. I'm glad that we got together,' I replied, 'and hope that we can do it together more often.'

'Which I hope so too,' he said, his hand moving down my back to grasp a cheek of my bum and give it a squeeze, 'for I just loved fucking your ass and having you fuck mine.'

***

WE KISSED and stroked each other for an hour before we were both again rampant and fucked each other again, getting the same pleasure as before at having our cum filling our backsides until we were both completely drained. It wasn't long after this that we rather reluctantly left the bed to get dressed and we promised to see to each other on a regular basis before I left and went to my flat to be there before Cyndi returned from work.

It was a normal husband and wife kiss when she arrived and I helped in preparing dinner after which, she wanted to go to bed early, which we did. I'm glad of those few hours respite from sex for I was then able to have the strength to bring her to two orgasms, one orally and the other the usual way by fucking her. Though I must admit that when I was up inside the heat of her vagina, I couldn't help thinking and comparing the difference of the fucking of Toby.

***

THREE DAYS later I had our front door bell ring which was an event for all the time I'd been there, this was the first time I had heard somebody press the button. I went and opened the door to a big surprise, for there stood Toby.

'Hello, John,' he said in a shy tone of voice. 'I thought you wouldn't mind if I visited you.'

'Not in the slightest, Toby. Come in, come in,' standing back to let him enter, and as soon as the door was shut, he was in my arms for us to kiss and press our groins up to each other, feeling that he was as hard as I was.

'I'm supposed to be visiting a client so I've got two hours,' he said breaking of the kiss. I led him through to the sitting room where he turned to face me.

'Can I take my clothes off, John? I like to be naked when I'm at home myself.'

'Of course,' I said, 'and I'll join you,' as I began taking my clothes off as he did so, letting me see that throbbing organ of his come into view, mine was acting the same and with us both naked, went into a clinch for our cocks to meet each other and rub themselves together as we kissed and tongued each other.

It was only a brief kiss we had before I went and put a disc in the player that showed a porn movie of two men having oral sex which we copied by laying down on the carpet in front of the screen, head to tail and avidly sucked and chewed on each other's rampant cock.

What bliss to have his pulsating piece of meat in my mouth again, tasting his love juice that I licked out of the eye of his cock. Making him shiver as I did when our tongues roved over the G-string with our hands moving slowly up and down the solid flesh that could be felt under the soft silky skin that covered it.

It didn't take long for us to reach our peak and joy of joys, had his cum erupt into my mouth, him getting mine at the same time. It was bliss to move this round in my mouth, pushing all over the head of his throbbing cock, getting another taste of him that was like nectar to me now. I finally swallowed it and loved the feeling of it all slide down my throat and with his cock still throbbing away in my mouth, knew that I also wanted this lovely hard cock up in my ass as I licked the head clean of his cum as he was doing to me before we released each other to turn round and kiss and get another taste of ourselves in the process.

'I really needed that, John,' he gasped out, 'and can't wait for you to fuck me with this lovely cock of yours

'And I want yours, Toby,' I said, kissing him again and began stroking his body as we did so. His hands were active in rubbing my back and going down to fondle the cheeks of my bum and it didn't take long with us fondling and sucking on each other's limp dicks did we rouse each other for them to become rampant cocks that wanted a hole to fuck.

It didn't take long to find the lube which I then feverishly coated the head of his cock and the entrance to my backside, not using my fingers inside for I wanted to really feel the pain of his entry, which I did when I was up on my knees in front of him. My body gave out a shiver when I felt the head of his cock nestle at the entrance to my ass and had that moment of pain when he widened it and I then had the glory of having his big prick enter and fill me with his thighs tight up to the cheeks of my ass.

I crooned at the soothing massage I was getting as I felt his pulsating cock slide back and forth, giving me the pleasure and thrill of once again having a rampant cock reaming me. The bonus to this, if it could be called that, was to see on the television the porn film where a man was fucking another man up the ass. I could see and feel what the man being fucked was feeling and revelled in the fact that Toby must have been watching it too for he was moving inside me at the same speed that was on the screen. There were two differences, they being that the man in the film was wearing a condom whereas Toby was fucking me bare back and that I was getting the extra thrill of feeling Toby's hands wandering up and down my sides and sometimes tweaking my nipples.

All this gave me another hard on and I had it bouncing up and down to Toby's movements, my balls swinging low beneath my now throbbing cock.

'Jerk me off, Toby,' I panted. 'Make me cum at the same time as you fill me with yours.' He leaned more on my rear end as his hand found and held my cock and started to move his hand in his firm grip. So not only was I having the pleasure of his cock up inside me, I was being jerked off at the same time. 'I'm getting there, Toby,' I gasped, and had his hand start to move faster and his hips moving more, slapping them against my bum cheeks, his balls now hitting mine as he did so.

'I'm cumming.....I'm cumming.....aaaaaah,' I cried as I started to shoot my load out onto the carpet and at the same time, felt his cum spurt into my ass, coating the canal which thrilled me as more came into me as I kept having my cum spray the carpet.

He came to a stop, his cock still throbbing away inside me as he leaned over my back, his heavy breathing quite loud and his hand left my dripping cock to come back up to my waist to help support him as he straightened himself up and began to pull out of me. I cried out at feeling his lovely organ starting to slip out of me and felt the cool air caress my shrinking hole when he left me, the one part of anal sex that I didn't like. The empty feeling of not having a throbbing cock pleasuring my insides, the pulsating hard piece of flesh taking me to heights that can only be called heaven, especially when it has smoothed out all the kinks and also creamed me at the same time.

We both rose up and went to the bathroom where we washed our cocks at the same time, grinning at each other's image in the mirror as we did so. Then back to the sitting room where we got dressed before going into a clinch to kiss and say how much we had enjoyed in having each other. It was agreed that I would go to his place next time for the same thrill of sucking and fucking each other, though he would have to phone me to say when he got the chance to slip out from work.

We would have our fun together at least twice a week over the next year until I found out that Cyndi had reverted back to her old self and started having sex with other men and women without me joining in. This led to another bust up of our marriage, for the second time, though I declared that this was the last straw and so I left her again and moved back to the town I had left. I stayed with some friends for a short while until I found a small apartment to move into.

Chapter Five

It had been a wrench to leave Toby, but that's life, for I couldn't live with Cyndi anymore. It didn't take me long in my new apartment to find a casual girlfriend who would stay over for a night of sex at odd times. As nice as it was, with me being bi-sexual, came to realise that I was turning more towards being a homosexual in that I would rather have a cock to suck and fuck me up the ass than fucking a woman.

So with only getting my end away at very infrequent times with this girl, I was getting desperate in wanting a man to fuck me. Not only to stick his cock up my ass but for me to suck on too, getting and tasting male cum to savour before swallowing. So I started cruising a few gay bars and it wasn't long before I met Charles. Like me, he lived alone and I found that he too wanted to fuck another man's ass and as we both seemed to get on well with each other in our talking at the bar while drinking, he agreed to come over to my place the coming Saturday, about 10 pm.

I laid in some beers and when he did arrive, on time, we went into my sitting room where we had a beer each before we got undressed to reveal that we both had erections. His was about the same size as mine, that being about seven inches when fully erect and I was quickly down on my knees before him to take hold of his throbbing cock and take the head into my mouth to suck. He was uncut and so with my lips firmly round the head, pushed his foreskin right down so that I had the bare flesh to suck and run my tongue round it, taking in the pearly drop of love juice from the eye of his cock before teasing the G-string. This made his body quiver with the erotic sensation this caused in him and soon had him groaning with delight.

'Not too much,' he begged. 'I'd rather have my cock up your ass.'

It was what I wanted too and so I let his cock head slip out of my mouth as I turned round to pick up the tube of lube and squeezing some out to cover his cock and put quite a big blob at the entrance to my backside before turning round again on my hands and knees to be ready for him to use that lovely cock inside me.

He quickly got behind me on his knees, pushing my legs further apart with his knees as he got himself into position and had a hand on my hip to steady himself. I couldn't stop the tremor in my body as I felt the head of his cock touch the blob of lube at my asshole and relaxed myself as much as possible when he started to push himself inside me. Without having used some lubed fingers inside me first, there was some pain as he stretched my opening, pausing with the head halfway in before moving a little bit more until the head suddenly slipped inside me. Oh what joy to feel it throb away and I used my muscle there to grip and squeeze as I flexed it before he pushed some more and then had the whole cock slide fully inside me till his thighs reached the cheeks of my bum and could go no further.

What a delight to once again have a pulsating cock slide back and forth inside me, massaging my canal and giving me all kinds of thrills as the head kept touching various nerves that are inside. With his hands firmly on my hips, he would pull me back onto every forward thrust of his cock into me, making my own erect cock bounce up and down and have my balls swing back and forth in his fucking of me.

'I'm not far off cumming,' Charles panted as he was reaming me and started to ram himself inside, making me drool at the mouth knowing I was going to feel his cum spray my insides. Not only that, when I felt that first surge do just that, my own cock let loose my cum to spray out onto the carpet as he cummed inside me. What a pleasure that was to feel his cum coat my channel as he kept up that forceful thrusting behind me, giving out a groan at every shot before coming to a stop and leaning over my rear end breathing heavily. I was panting as well as I came until there was only a dribble of my cum hanging from the end of my cock.

I gave out a cry as he pulled out of me, flexing my muscle to try and hold him there, but to no avail and it slipped out for me to feel the cool air move round my shrinking asshole. I rolled over onto my back, my dripping wet cock flopping onto my stomach leaving a trail of cum up my upper thigh as it was still hanging there from the head of my cock.

I watched that lovely fucking organ sway about as he got up and went off to the bathroom to wash himself and I glowed inside with the pleasure I had just received and had more to come when he came back into the sitting room. He got back down onto his knees between my legs and began to lick up my cum from my thigh before taking the head into his mouth to suck out any more that I still had inside it. Not only sucking that out but licking all over the head until I was clean.

We stayed lying naked on the carpet for nearly an hour, drinking our beer and talking and learned that Charles was only in town for this last day but would be returning later in the month and would like to come again for sex as he enjoyed his evening so far.

'In fact, I'm ready now,' he said, which was obvious to me as I had been stroking his cock and it was now hard in my hand. 'Roll over onto your knees.'

This I did, spreading my legs for him to get in between them and got a small shock as I felt him kiss the cheeks of my bum before his hands spread them apart and felt his tongue run up the crease and tickle my rosebud. This sent tingles throughout my body and literally crooned when his tongue was inserted inside me during his licking and kissing of me there.

'Pass me the lube,' he said, his voice sounding a little hoarse. 'I think that it was a bit painful with your asshole not being opened up first.' Which indeed it had been, but it was a small price to pay for the pleasure he had given me. With the lube, he obviously had put some on his finger for that was what was pushed up into my ass. Not as good as a cock but still nice to have one moving inside me. I gave out a little cry when he pulled it out but it was to lube another finger and so had two pushed back inside me, moving about and making my asshole relax a bit more and even had three fingers in me eventually.

'Okay. Roll over onto your back,' he said after he'd pulled them out. This I did and watched him put more lube all over the head of his cock which looked really powerful as it bounced about, his big balls swinging beneath it. Loving that sac that held the cum that I was going to have inside me in a few minutes. With the lube put to one side, he lifted up my legs and put them up onto his shoulders as he shuffled forward, partly lifting my backside up off the floor. His eyes were bright and shining and I smiled back at him and gave out shiver as I felt the head of his cock rub up against the entrance to my body. He held it there for a moment as he settled my legs on his shoulders, his hands holding me by the knees as he smiled down at me and then pushed forward.

What a joy to now watch the expression on his face as I felt the head of his cock widen my lubricated ring piece, as well as getting the pleasure of him entering me again. He slipped in more easily this time to just a slight pain that was soon smoothed out as the head moved inside, throbbing away and had the rest of his big cock fully enter until his thighs were tight up to the cheeks of my bum. It was pure bliss to feel him pulsating inside me as he began to fuck me with that lovely hard cock.

He held my legs firmly as he moved in his fucking of me, his balls smacking my bum with every forward thrust which was the added thrill knowing that he was stirring up the sperm that would shortly be cumming inside me. My own cock was as hard as an iron bar throbbing up on my stomach and with my arms outstretched, I could only just stroke his hands as he fucked me. With him cumming only an hour before, this time he lasted a bit longer which pleased me, flexing my muscle with each and every thrusting of his rampant cock inside me.

But nature took over and it wasn't long before he started to really pull me up onto him as he rammed himself forward, making his cock really twitch inside me and he didn't have to say that he was about to cum. And cum he did! The cock head swelled a bit more as his first salvo erupted inside me, giving me the thrill of feeling it hit and coat the walls of my canal making me drool with the pleasure of having his cum come inside me. Not one shot but six, though coming with not as much force as the first one but strong enough to be felt.

He came to a stop, panting hard, a big smile on his face as he made his cock twitch to try and get the last of his cum out of the eye of his cock, me helping by squeezing his shaft with my inside muscle.

'Oh, Charles, that was just great, man! Just great,' I said, looking up at him and smiling.

'That it was, John. Pure heaven,' he replied and began to pull out.

'Noooo,' I cried as I felt it leaving my asshole, that tool of pleasure, my totem, the phallic God that I now really knew that I worshipped. He gave out a grunt as it left my ass, easing my legs off his shoulders to slip down the sides of his body as he moved backwards and lay down between them. His arms came up over my hips and lifted up my now really throbbing cock and pulled it back a little to take the head into his mouth.

I loved male sex. Being fucked by a man and now having my cock sucked and teased by his tongue as his hand moved the outer skin up and down in a firm grasp. It wasn't long before I was crying out that I was about to come for he would surely have felt my thighs tightening up and the head of my cock swelling that little bit more. His hand tightened up as he helped my cum shoot out of the eye into his mouth in steady shots, colliding with what was already there, joining up again as it had been in my balls.

He swallowed all this in one go before squeezing the head again to get the last drops out before licking all over the exposed flesh before slithering up my body till he was fully on top of me to kiss and pass over what was left of my cum into my mouth as we did so.

'What nectar you produce,' he said. 'An Ambrosia that is a pleasure to taste. I wish all those that I've sucked before had tasted like yours.'

'I wish that other men had a cock like yours,' I answered, 'for it's the best I've ever had.' I smiled up at him, not minding his weight on me as we kissed again before we finally broke apart for him to roll off onto his back.

We had another beer as we talked, him wanting to see me again when he was next back in town and I gave him my phone number which he promised to ring me in advance of when that would be. We then got dressed and after another kiss by the front door of my flat, he left.

***

IT WAS several days later that I made contact with Larry on Yahoo Messenger. He had been cruising the net the same as me, looking for a likely person who had the same proclivity as myself in wanting male sex. We chatted for a little while and then agreed that he should come round to my flat which he did. He was about the same height as me, dark hair, blue eyes and about the same weight as me and was a really good looking young man, several years younger than me.

It was a tentative handshake he gave me at the door when we first set eyes on each other and it wasn't until he was inside and the door shut that I took him into my arms and we kissed for the first time. That broke the ice and I led him into the sitting room where I sat him down, putting a porno DVD on the player before getting us some beers. We drank some watching males having sex on the screen as I began stroking the front of his trousers, feeling that he was hard already. He then stroked mine to find that I was in the same state that he was in.

'Let's get these clothes off,' I said and we both got up and quickly took them off for me to see that his erect cock was at least eight and a half inches in length and quite big at the base. He looked at mine and smiled before we went into each other's arms to kiss and tongue each other, our erect cocks clashing and getting squashed between us as we explored our mouths with our tongues. We were both panting when we broke off the kiss and I pushed him back to sit down on the sofa, his cock standing out proud from his groin.

I gave out a groan as I wanted that lovely looking big cock in both places and went down onto my knees and spread apart his legs to move in between them. With my elbows on his thighs, I took hold of his erect cock, feeling it throbbing in my hand as I gave it a rub and squeezed the head to make the eye open. Into this I blew a stream of my breath and made him give out a shudder before I opened my mouth, bending my head, and took it inside.

My body tingled as I took it in, pushing the foreskin down with my lips so that I had the bare flesh to tongue, which I did, running it all over that solid meat and teased the G-string that made his body quiver at the erotic sensations that I knew he was getting. It was hot and like solid rubber as I gently chewed it while I sucked, in heaven that I once again had a man's cock in my mouth to savour. As much as I wanted to taste, savour and swallow his cum, my butt was itching to have this lovely organ up inside my ass.

I let him go to a gasp from him as I reached for the lube which I had put there earlier, and squeezed some out to coat the head and shaft of his wonderful hard cock and put some too at the entrance to my backside.

'Fuck me with this, Larry,' I said in a hoarse voice, giving it one more rub before turning round on the carpet on my hands and knees, letting him see the target he was to aim at and fill with his powerful looking weapon. I didn't see him rise from the sofa but felt his hand come onto my hip and his knees nudge my legs further apart. I was already drooling at the mouth as I felt the head of his cock touch and be held firm at the entrance to my asshole.

Without being lubed properly, there was a little pain as he began to widen the orifice of my ass as he pushed himself forward, but I was now used to this and welcomed it as the prelude to the pleasure that would override the initial pain and gave out a sigh when the head slipped in and then gurgled as the rest of his eight and a half inches smoothly slid inside me, feeling it throb and pulsate as it did so.

I was in heaven again at having the hard flesh of another man's come up into my ass and flexed my muscle there round the solid flesh as it moved inside me. What bliss to have his hands on my hips as his big cock smoothly moved back and forth inside me, ironing out any kinks and soothing the itch that I had there for such a cock as his. I found I was crooning as he slid back and forth, loving the feel of him moving inside me as well as having his balls smack my lower bum cheeks as his thighs came firm up to those cheeks.

'Harder, Larry! Ram it in! Really fuck me!' I cried out and went into a state of euphoria as he did so, ramming himself hard into me, loving the power that I felt in his cock as it reamed my back passage. But by him doing this soon brought him to his peak and with even harder thrusts of his cock into me he then held me in a firm grip as I felt him start to send his cum up into my ass.

Oh what pleasure that was to feel his cum coating my canal as shot after shot spurted inside me till he came to a full stop, leaning over my rear end as he panted away and I swear I felt drops of sweat land on my back as he did so. But then came the hated part of sex this way as I felt him lean back and his still hard cock slowly starting to leave my body. I gave out a little cry as I tried to hold him there with my inside muscle, but alas, to no avail and had that wonderful fucking tool leave my ass. Cool air rushed into that now vacant orifice for nature abhorred a vacuum before it had time to shrink back to its normal closed state.

I went and rolled over onto my back, my cock lying flat on my stomach. I don't think I've mentioned it before but in its flaccid state, my cock is four and half inches in length but when fully aroused, it measures seven inches, and this was now lying there until I lifted it upright, smiling up at Larry who was still on his knees.

He smiled back at me and licked his lips before moving in between my open legs, lying full length on the carpet, moved my hand off of my cock and took it in his and began to slowly rub it up and down. This stretched my foreskin halfway down the head and with another licking of his lips, bent his head down and took the head of my cock into his mouth, pushing the foreskin down as I had done to his.

His mouth was hot as he engulfed me and made me quiver as his tongue found the G-string while caressing the head as he gently chewed at it. It didn't take long with his hand firmly moving up and down on the shaft, the skin moving smoothly over the solid flesh that it covered. His mouth sucking away as his tongue roved over the bare flesh was rousing me up to the point of cumming, and cum is what erupted out of the eye of my cock. I'm sure that first surge hit the roof of his mouth for I heard what sounded like a strangled cough but the next shot was of a lesser force and he took that without a sound as he did for the rest. My cum filling his mouth which he swallowed, knowing that he had from that extra little suction I felt round the head of my cock.

He kept on sucking until I was empty and then stroked his tongue all round to clean off any residue before letting me free of that lovely mouth of his. He grinned up at me before he slid up my body until he was fully on top of me as we kissed. The bugger had also kept some of my cum in his mouth for he managed to push it into mine though it not being the first time that I had tasted my own cum. I had quite often masturbated to have my cum come into my hand for me to suck up and then lick off the rest afterwards. Though the best taste was really the love juice that preceded my cumming, for it tasted like sweet clear honey.

But we'd finished our first sexual encounter and on getting up from the carpet, sat back on the couch and drank some beer, telling each other how wonderful it had been and that when we were up to strength again, it would be me fucking him and then me sucking on him. This we did, much to the pleasure of both of us and when finished, agreed to have a regular session at least once a week which we did for quite some time.

Chapter Six

It was a couple of weeks later when cruising the gay bars again when I met Bob. Now we had met before when I was with Charles but that was only to say hello to at the time, but this time I was on my own. He had guessed that Charles and I were an item so to speak but that didn't stop us from having a chat together.

'So you've been and fucked with Charles then?' he asked a short while into our conversation as we sat at the bar.

'Yes,' I admitted.

'So have I,' he said, 'though only the once. We, er, well, didn't really hit it off as a couple. I saw you in here when you first met him and went off with him. Why are you in here again?'

'Well, I'm at a bit of a loose end looking for another loose end,' I said, pointedly looking at his crotch. He saw where I was looking and smiled as I saw that he was actually growing inside his trousers.

'I've got a loose end that needs to be attached to someone,' he smiled at me as he rubbed his growing member. His smile was lovely to see, his teeth nice and white showing between his lips. Lips that I suddenly had an urge to kiss. Not only kiss but be around the head of my cock and what with him wanting somewhere to put his loose end as he called it, I started getting hard inside my trousers. Now it was him looking at what was happening to me.

'Say no more, Bob. Would you like to come over to my place? It's not far from here,' I said and got that smile again.

'I sure would like that, John,' he said, and so we finished our beers and left the bar.

It was only ten minutes later that we were inside my flat and as soon as the door was closed, we were kissing each other as our hands fondled the front of our trousers.

'You feel big, Bob,' I said between our kisses, still rubbing his hard erection that was still hidden from sight.

'I was just about to say the same thing, John,' him rubbing me the same way.

'Well, let's see if we've come up to our expectations,' I said, leading him into the sitting room.

It didn't take long before we had stripped our clothes off and stood facing each other, naked, and both with our erect cocks sticking out in front of us. I moved first and went down onto my knees and took the head of his lovely looking cock into my mouth. He was about the same size as me and it easily fitted into my mouth for me to suck, for the first time, a cut cock, him not having a foreskin. But he still had his G-string which I tickled with my tongue making his body quiver as I did so.

'Let's do it together,' he said, his voice sounding a little hoarse as he pulled his cock head out of my mouth. This I wanted too, having just licked off his love juice. He saw that I had some coming out of the eye of my cock and took this off with his finger and put it in his mouth. 'Delicious,' he said, as I then took hold of his cock and led him by it into my bedroom where I had to let go as we got onto the bed.

He went into the opposite position to me and we rolled onto our sides presenting our rigid cocks to our open mouths. It was grand to not only have his cock inside for me to suck and chew on but have him doing the same to me. We sucked, chewed, tongued and teased each other until our senses could take no more and were soon trying to ram the whole lengths of our cocks into each other's mouth.

It was only by holding the cock in front of us that stopped us from choking each other as we both started to give each other our cum, and cum we did. Load after load he shot into my mouth, him getting the same from me, which we finally swallowed when we'd finished cumming.

'You sure taste good, John,' he said after he had turned round on the bed so that we could kiss and fondle each other.

'The same goes for you, Bob,' I replied, opening my mouth again in another kiss so that our tongues could play with each other. Not only our tongues but our hands as well, stroking down the waist and moving the soft penis to be able to hold the balls of each other. These were moved around in their sac, being done gently so as not to ruin what they produced inside.

It wasn't long before I felt his finger being pushed up into my ass, guessing that he wanted to widen me for later fucking me when he was up and rampant again. I broke off the kissing to turn and get a tube of lube out of the bedside drawer and pass it over to him as I started fondling his still limp cock in my hand. He lubed his finger and soon had it up inside my ass and a few minutes later it was two working away in my asshole. It was turning us both on, our cocks getting harder every minute. Me wanting his cock where his fingers were and him wanting to put it there too as he finished up with four fingers there and knew I was ready to be fucked.

He sat up, his cock now up and hard as iron as he then pushed me onto my back and moved himself in between my legs that I opened up for him. I lifted them up and he held the calves and got my heels up over his shoulders as he moved in closer, his cock bouncing nicely and I began to drool at seeing what I was about to have shoved up inside me. He lifted me up a little more so that my heels could lock behind his neck as I felt the head of his cock touch the entrance to my ass and sighed when he moved and had the head enter me.

It was lovely even just having the head widen me that little bit more, the pain negligible as it throbbed inside me. His eyes were shining as he smiled at me, not moving as I flexed my muscle round the head of his cock, making it twitch.

'Push, Bob, push and fuck me,' I begged and had him do just that. It was cool man, having that throbbing cock slide fully inside me, making all the nerves tingle till his thighs were tight up to the cheeks of my bum. 'Lovely,' I crooned as he began to move that wonderful organ backwards and forwards, reaming my channel with his hard cock. I was in heaven again at having him fuck and excite my whole body with his fucking of me, making my own cock throb as it gently bounced on my stomach.

He had been moving slowly inside me, trying to make the pleasure for both of us last longer, which it did up to a point where nature took over and soon had him ramming himself into me, feeling his balls smack my bum and making my cock really bounce up and down. It was when his own body went rigid with only his hips jerking slightly that I had his first load of cum spray my insides. Feeling it hit me, made my own cock let go and I had my cum come shooting out of the eye to spray itself right the way up my chest and under my chin. One long stream of cum that felt hot to my skin only to be followed by more, cumming at the same time as Bob was until I had one long trail of cum from my navel up to my throat.

His cum inside me was better than lube as it made his cock slide that more easily inside me as he tried to really empty his balls in his last violent stabs at me before coming to a halt. He was breathing as heavily as me as we both smiled at each other. My legs now slipping off his shoulders, the action making him start to slide out of me. I gave out a cry and tried to hold him there by clenching my buttocks tighter than ever, but he slipped out in spite of my trying to prevent this loss of that wonderful reaming cock of his.

He moved back a little before falling forward between my legs, his face just above my cock which he then lifted up and began to suck out any residue of cum that was still inside it. With it empty and the head cleaned off by his tongue, he pushed it to one side and began to lick his way up my body, taking all the cum up off my stomach and chest as he moved ever so slowly up till he had taken it all in to taste and swallow before lying fully on top of me for us to kiss and share some of my cum that he had held back in his mouth.

That was our first cumming together and after having had a shower, we got dressed and kissed each other goodbye before he left. It wasn't our only sex between us for he would then come over nearly every weekend and at odd week days though he would always let me know first, just in case I had Charles or someone else with me.

***

ONE DAY, Bob sent over a text asking if I would be home all day and if so, could he come over? I immediately sent back a text saying that I would be waiting for him and would have a surprise for him.

Not knowing how long he would be, I was quickly in the shower getting myself clean and then I went and shaved all the hair off my body except for my head and a thin line from my cock up to my stomach until my body was as smooth as silk. I then rummaged through some of the clothes that my occasional girlfriend had left at my flat and put some of them on. All this had taken time, nearly two hours and was only just ready when the doorbell rang. It was Bob, and his face showed his surprise at what I was wearing.

This female attire was a denim mini skirt that only came down to my mid thighs, a tank top that left my midriff bare and a pair of panties to keep my erection flat to my stomach and not push out the front of the skirt. The surprise look stayed on his face as he took me into his arms and kissed me, not only kiss but tried to deep throat me with his tongue.

He said, after us breaking apart, that I looked fabulous, remarking on the smoothness of my skin as he ran a hand up and down my upper leg. I could see that he was aroused by the bulge in his trousers, a bulge that I wanted out in the open for me to suck and play with.

I led him into the sitting room and made him sit down on the couch while I went into the kitchen to fetch us a beer each and then went and sat down next to him. After only a few swigs at his can, his hand began moving up and down the inside of my upper thigh which aroused me at the thrill of being dressed as I was and having him stroke my hairless legs. I had no objections when he pulled me into his arms for us to kiss, his hand taking mine and putting it to the front of his trousers for me to feel that he was hard and ready for me.

It was a bit difficult for me to undo his belt with one hand, but I managed and was then able to pull down the zipper and put my hand inside his trousers and pull out that lovely throbbing organ. The bare fleshed head was almost purple in colour with the blood pulsating up and round his cock and I gave it a squeeze to make the eye appear to wink at me before I kissed it. Then I took the whole head into my hot mouth to begin to suck and gently chew on, not forgetting to tongue the G-string to make his body quiver at the erotic sensation that it caused.

As I sucked on him, his hand was active and was under the skirt and moving under my panties until he was able to get a finger up into my ass. This made me tremble and eased myself up, letting his cock fall free from my mouth as I let him pull these panties off and I passed him the lube to cover his fingers before I took the head of his cock back into my mouth. Now with his fingers lubed, I had then one at a time being pushed into my ass until I had all four of them widen my asshole to accommodate the cock I was still sucking on.

'Let's get these clothes off so that we can fuck properly,' he said, his fingers leaving my ass and pulling his cock from my mouth. So standing up, we quickly took our clothes off and he looked at me taking the skirt off said, 'Is it John or Joanne that I'm going to fuck?' he asked with a smile.

'Both,' I grinned back at him giving out a chuckle that really sounded like a girlish giggle as I finished up as naked as he was, both of us with a raging stalk sticking out from our groins.

He noted then that round my erection I was hairless except for that thin strip and he gave out a whistle as he stroked all round where there had once been hair, even my balls which he said he would like to suck, which he did there and then by dropping down onto his knees. His nose pushed up my throbbing cock and had the glorious thrill of having both of my balls in his mouth to be sucked and teased as he moved them round in their sac. If he'd kept that up, I would have cummed all over his head, but he didn't and so we went into the bedroom where I went and lay on my back with my legs open for him to get in between them.

It was a sight for sore eyes and a quivering asshole to see that cock bounce about as he lifted my legs up to his shoulders before moving in closer until his cock disappeared from sight but was felt to touch my ring piece. I lifted my bum up a little and had him then lean forward and had his cock move into my expanded hole to give me that thrill of once again having a throbbing cock move up into my ass. It was lovely to have him moving himself in and out of me and then I had a sudden craving to suck him after having had him up my ass.

'Pull out for a minute, Bob, for I want to have a suck on you again before you cum inside me,' I said. He looked a little surprised at me wanting to suck on him after having it where it was now.

He had come to a sudden stop at my request but now he let my legs slip off his shoulders as he pulled out and then moved up the bed to straddle me and helped hold my head up for me to take the head of his cock back into my mouth after it just coming out from my backside. This really is a no-no act, but I was just being perverse in wanting it at this moment in time. I then got a taste of my anal juice but not of his pre cum for that had been wiped off in my ass.

It was only for a couple of minutes that I sucked but it was enough, besides, my neck was beginning to hurt in that position. So with letting it go, he moved back down and lifted my legs up again so that he could carry on in his fucking of me.

His cock slipped easily back into my ass, much to my delight, and had him again reaming with his in and out movement, thrilling me even more as I felt the head of his cock swell up and had him shoot his cum inside me. Shot after shot, coating my insides, making my body tingle all over, especially with that lovely smile he gave me when he'd finished cumming. My legs slid down off his shoulders and he lay between my legs with his cock still twitching inside me until it got so soft that it slipped out of its own accord.

I couldn't help but give out a sob when this happened, and Bob was quick to move up to half lay on me as he first kissed my eye lids that had a few drops of tears formed there before kissing me on the lips oh so gently before speaking.

'I didn't hurt you, John, did I?' he asked, pity in his eyes. I clung to him and buried my head in his shoulder, the tears now running down my face as I sobbed.

'No, Bob. It didn't hurt. It's....it's just the loss of that wonderful cock of yours from inside me. I so do love it when it is throbbing away inside me, especially when you cum and I hate it when it's pulled out.'

'Well, it won't be long before it's back in there for I just love putting it in you, giving both of us the pleasure of it being there and me cumming,' he said, stroking my head before moving it back for him to kiss me.

That was then for the first time, I felt like a woman recalling the thrill I had got when I had put on that skirt and tank top and now having just been fucked as one. I clutched him and fiercely kissed him before moving down the bed and sucking on his limp cock. This I did till I raised him back up into a fucking mode and welcomed him back inside me once again to give me the pleasure of having that throbbing hard flesh reaming my insides and having him shoot his cum once more into my ass. I kept him inside of me again until it wilted and slipped out but didn't cry this time.

Time had flown by and he said that he had to go and so we parted from our kissing and we got off the bed and both had a shower before he got dressed while I stayed naked. He kissed me again, stroking my bare back and the cheeks of my bum that still had some of his cum slowly seeping out and running down my inner thigh.

'I love your hairless body and next time I come, I want you to wear the skirt and things for it roused me quicker than just seeing you.' Then he was gone and I was once again all on my own.

Chapter Seven

Next day it was back to surfing the web when I'd finished my own work on the computer and made contact with a guy named Glenn. He was avid for sex and so I invited him over to my place and he duly turned up the next day. He was tall, about five eleven and quite well built, brown hair and eyes of the same colour and white teeth which showed when he smiled.

I took him into the sitting room where he sat on the couch while I fetched us some beers and we chatted for a while, telling each other of our work etc. Until we both ran out of things to say, our eyes steady as we looked at each other and I started the ball rolling by pulling him into my arms and kissing him. From that point there was no stopping us, kissing, tonguing and stroking the front of each other's trousers, feeling the erect and hard cock inside them.

Our clothes were soon off and with us naked, he pushed me down onto the couch and got down on his knees between mine and took the head of my cock into his mouth. It was grand having myself inside that hot mouth as I watched his head bob up and down as he sucked and chewed on me till I went slightly rigid and began bucking my hips upwards as I sent my cum spurting out to fill his mouth.

He looked up at me when I'd finished cumming, his eyes sparkling as he lifted his head and showed me the mouthful of my cum that he had held there and I watched him swallow it before he bent down again to lick the head of my cock clean. He sat back on his heels, his cut cock sticking out proud from his groin.

'Will you suck on me now?' he asked. A silly question really for that was why he was here, for us to suck each other first and then fuck. I moved off the couch for him to sit down and I took hold of his seven-inch cock, looking at the bare flesh after being circumcised before taking it into my mouth. It was hot, throbbing and hard and I had great pleasure in the gentle chewing of it as I sucked. It wasn't long before he said he was cumming and had my mouth filled with his cum and did the same at showing him what he had given me before swallowing his load that tasted quite nice.

I got some more beers from the kitchen to drink while sitting on the couch waiting for us both to rise up again, which eventually happened, and so putting down our empty cans, I led him into the bedroom. He said that he wanted to fuck me first, in the doggie position which I didn't mind at all and passed him the lube and got onto the bed on my knees. I watched him cover his cock with the lube and had him coat his fingers as well which he then put inside the hole of my ass and gave me a thrill at having them move as they started to widen me for his thick seven-inch cock.

'Now, Glenn, now,' I begged after several minutes of him playing with my asshole with his fingers, 'let me have that cock of yours there instead of the fingers.' He quickly pulled them out and got in between my legs and held my hips as I felt the head of his cock nestle itself at the entrance to my ass.

It was lovely to once again have a cock slide in and fill me with pleasure and joy, his hands firmly on my hips as he began to ride me, pulling me back onto his forward thrusting as his cock slid smoothly backwards and forwards. I was loving the massage he was giving me, tickling me in some places that made me tingle with the joy of having him there, fucking me.

'This is great,' he said as he shafted me. 'I haven't had such a tight ass to fuck before, it's great,' and started to ram himself harder into me and soon went rigid and I felt him start to send his cum up into me. Oh what bliss to feel it spurt and spray my insides as he came, filling me with his cum and joy. He came to a stop, leaning over my backside, apologising for cumming too soon, saying it was the tightness of my ass that made this happen so quickly. But what the fuck! That was the whole purpose of fucking an ass and that was to cum inside it, giving us both the pleasure in the doing of it.

I gave out that little cry when he pulled out and went off into the bathroom to wash himself while I lubed up my now really throbbing cock, having seen the cheeks of his arse move sedately to the bathroom. When he came back, he smiled at seeing me up and rampant to service him and he assumed the same position that I had on the bed for me to get in between his legs behind him. I didn't lube my fingers for I wanted him to feel the real me forcing my way up into his ass and having pulled the cheeks of his bum apart, saw my target and quickly shoved my cock into his hole.

I was in so quick that his sphincter muscle didn't have time to react to this intrusion and he gave out a loud gasp as I filled his ass with my pulsating cock, pushing right in until my thighs were tight up to the cheeks, my balls slapping against his as I came to a stop. I began ploughing his field where I was going to plant my seed, making furrow after furrow as I moved back and forth before, and like him, came too soon and began pumping my cum out into the furrows I had ploughed, knowing that my seed would not fertilise this open meadow.

'Wow! You sure know how to fuck, John,' he gasped as I came to a full stop after giving him all of my cum. 'I don't think I've had better.' His muscle was constantly flexing itself round the whole of my shaft making my cock twitch inside him. As much as I liked in the fucking of him, there was no point in staying there as I didn't have any cum left to give him, so I pulled out to hear the same cry that I always gave when a lovely fucking organ was removed from my backside.

I went off into the bathroom to wash myself and he followed me in, asking if he could have a shower as he didn't want to have the smell of sex on him when he went home to his wife. This I agreed to and after he'd cleaned off our smells, dried and got dressed, we kissed each other saying what a wonderful afternoon it had been and he would look forward to another session in the near future.

***

A COUPLE of weeks later I got an e-mail from Charles saying that he would be coming to town the next day and would it be okay if his buddy, David, could come too for making it a threesome in the afternoon about half past five. I e-mailed straight back saying yes and that it would be just great. Tingles went up and down my spine as I wrote this and got a massive hard on right there and then and so just had to jerk myself off at the thought of three of us fucking and sucking each other. I had this picture in my mind as I worked my hand up and down on my cock and managed to control the spurts of my cum into my hand for me to lick off and swallow before cumming again to suck off, cumming six times and swallowing the lot, licking my hand and fingers clean afterwards. Well, it was the best I could do on my own!

They turned up on time and I welcomed them both in and got a full on the lips kiss from Charles and a shy peck on the cheek from his friend David. I told them to sit down in the sitting room while I got some beers out from the kitchen and on returning, saw that Charles was already taking his clothes off.

'Come on, David,' he said, taking a can of beer from me. 'The norm here is to be naked, so show John what you've got for him this afternoon.'

I got a shy smile from David as he put his can of beer down and started to get undressed, me doing the same until all three of us were naked and drinking our beer. We all had an erect cock and I noticed that David's was a bit bigger than that of Charles, but neither of them as big as mine, sticking up from my thighs for them to see that I was ready for sex.

I finished my beer first and was quickly over to where David and Charles were sitting on the couch, and went down onto my knees to take the head of Charles' cock into my mouth. He gave out a groan as I did so and quickly finished his beer and pushed my head up from sucking his lovely hard cock.

'Enough of sucking on me,' he said. 'Give David a suck and let me fuck you.' A suggestion I wasn't going to refuse, getting a glow in my stomach at the prospect of two cocks being inside me. I quickly shuffled over to get between the open legs of David and took hold of his throbbing cock, giving the thing a big squeeze making the eye open up into which I blew some air that really made him quiver and his cock twitch. I took that pulsating head in, pushing his foreskin down with my lips and made him give out a groan at feeling my tongue move round to tickle his G-string as I felt the hands of Charles part the cheeks of my bum. I had seen him lube up his cock that I now felt starting to probe the entrance to my ass and simply loved to feel the head start to expand my ring piece as he pushed forward.

What joy it was to have a throbbing cock in my mouth and feel another one open up my ass and slide in, filling me with pleasure and knowing that I would soon be filled with cum too. With Charles then moving me forward in his fucking of me, I was being pushed in my sucking of David's nice cock, even being able to take the whole thing in for it to touch my throat as my nose got buried into his pubic hair. My own cock was now a solid bar of flesh that was bouncing up and down and my balls swinging as Charles really started to ram himself into my ass. I managed to get my hand round the base of David's cock to start jerking him off for I wanted the cum of both of them to shoot into me at the same time.

Well, it was close enough to feel the first salvo of Charles spray my inside channel and the second one before David's thighs tightened up and he began jerking his hips up towards me as his cum shot into my mouth. My heart was pounding away in my chest and I had a lovely glow in my stomach as I was being filled with cum at both ends of my body, loving the feel of it coming inside my ass and loving the taste of that in my mouth.

With Charles leaning over my back when he'd finished cumming, panting away, I lifted my head up from David's cock to see his smiling face looking down at me and it got wider as he saw that I had all of his cum in my mouth that I had open for him to see before I swallowed it and went back down on him to lick the head of his cock clean.

I gave out my usual little cry as I felt Charles pulling his cock out of my ass, to get up and go off to the bathroom to wash himself as I pulled away from David's cock. I got him to get up from the couch and down onto his knees in front of me, showing me his backside and the tight cheeks of his bum that I parted to see the hole that I now wanted to tongue.

I bent my head and began to run my tongue up the crack of his ass making him quiver and then give out a jerk as he felt my tongue dart into his hole during my rimming of him. I was still doing this when Charles came back into the room and going and sitting down on the couch. His cock was now semi hard laying in between his thighs and this made David move round to take it into his mouth to try and raise it up to its fighting strength again.

I got hold of the lube and covered the head of my cock with it as I looked at the ass of David that I was going to fuck, and this I did, moving behind and between his open legs, gently eased my cock into his ass, his body trembling as I widened his asshole before the head slipped in. I paused then for a moment as his muscle flexed itself round the head and knew that he would be able to take the lot in as I then pushed forward till I was fully inside with my thighs up against his bum cheeks.

His inner body was hot and tight, just as I liked an ass and so I fucked David as he sucked on Charles. As much as I loved fucking another man, realised then that of the two, I'd rather be the one taking a cock up my ass being fucked than doing the fucking, but sex was in the giving as well as the taking, and so ploughed this, for me, fresh field and eventually held his hips tight as I gave him my cumming. He grunted at every shot, well that was all he could do with having his mouth filled with the cock of Charles.

Having filled his ass with my cum, I slowly pulled out, feeling his muscle trying to hold me there, but out I came to a noise that sounded like a fart and went off to the bathroom to wash myself. When I returned, they had changed positions and it was now David on his knees with Charles fucking him up the ass. David gave me a big smile as I saw them in this act and knew that David was enjoying it for his cock was quite stiff, bouncing up and down to the fucking movements of Charles. Even though I hadn't long cummed, my cock started getting hard again and went down onto the carpet and laying on my back, shuffled my way underneath David and took his bouncing cock into my mouth to suck.

Charles was panting as he fucked David who was grunting at every forward thrust of that cock up his ass and I was gurgling at the delight of having the cock of David sliding back and forth in my mouth.

'I'm cumming......I'm cumming,' cried out Charles, moving faster in his fucking of David's ass until he held the body up tight to his thighs as he began pumping out his cum.

'So am I.....cumming,' David got out with his gasping breath and I was delighted in being the recipient of having his cum start shooting into my mouth. What a delight it was to have my mouth filled again with a bucket full of cum, well it felt that much as I had a job to hold it all there till he'd finished emptying his balls. Only then did I swallow this nectar of the gods and lifting my head again to lick the head of his cock clean.

What a delighted and satisfied trio we were after this, getting up to sit on the couch for another beer with David as Charles went and washed himself, joining us after he had cleaned himself up. It took us a little while to gather our strength again for another session so that we'd each been fucked twice as well as being sucked when it was time for them to leave. I stayed naked as they got dressed and got a kiss from both as they fondled my cock with a kiss as we said our goodbyes and thanked them for coming, grinning at the pun.

But I was then left all alone again, wondering who and when would I have a rampant cock to fuck me and fill me with cum, such as what was now slowly oozing out of my ass and sliding down my inner thighs.

Chapter Eight

It was a couple of weeks later that Charles sent me another e-mail saying that he would be in town the next day and would be with me around noon time. He did add that he was alone this time. I replied saying that he would be welcomed and that it was a pity that David wouldn't be with him and I would leave the door unlocked for him as well as have a surprise that I think he would like.

What I was going to do was dress up as I had done for Glenn, and so next morning I really cleaned myself in the shower, making sure that the hole of my ass was as clean as it could be and shaved myself again before putting on the tank top, the mini skirt and panties and was sitting down at my computer when he arrived.

I heard the front door close and so closed down my computer and stood up as he entered the sitting room and gave me a wide smile when he saw what I was wearing. He quickly came over and took me into his arms to kiss me, feeling that the sight of me had aroused him, his cock hard inside his trousers. Mind you, I was just as hard inside the panties I was wearing.

'You look really fabulous,' he said after breaking off the kiss and holding me at arm's length as he looked up and down at my body before pulling me to him for another kiss, this time with his hands running down over the cheeks of my bum inside the skirt, squeezing them at the same time. 'You feel hot,' he said, breaking off the kiss again and pulling up the bottom of the tank top and pulled it over my head and threw it onto the couch.

He bent his head and started to kiss a nipple on my chest and I then noticed, really for the first time, that I appeared to have developed small breasts. I must have more female hormones than a male, was my thoughts, looking down at the tight and upright nipple on the breast that he wasn't sucking on. It was only a small breast, but one nonetheless, so maybe it was these hormones that made me want a male cock fucking my ass and having the cum fill me all the time.

This I knew I wanted and couldn't wait for him to stop kissing and sucking on my nipples for me to drag him into the bedroom where he stripped off his clothes as I took off the skirt and panties before getting onto the bed, our cocks clashing against each other as we embraced in yet another kiss. The word kiss is a misnomer really for they were really tongue games as they played with each other as well as being sucked, though I also liked it when his tongue was rimming my asshole.

This he did before rolling me over onto my back and lifting my legs up onto his shoulders and leaning in towards me. I gave out a shiver as I felt the head of his cock touch the entrance to my ass and smiled up him as he teased me with it.

'Fuck me, Charles. Blow my fucking brains out,' I begged him, and got a smile from him as I then felt the head of his cock slowly start to expand my hole, giving me a little pain for he hadn't lubed himself, but in spite of that lack, the head slipped in and he held it there at the entrance, throbbing away and making all of my insides churn and quiver at the feel of him once again about to fill me with his lovely cock and then later, his cum. 'Don't tease me, you bugger! Fuck me!' I cried, and he did just that. He pulled my thighs tighter to his body as the rest of his cock, that hard shaft being pushed in to fill me with what our sex was all about. Having it up my ass and giving me the pleasure of having a male organ smoothing out the kinks inside my canal.

What a fuck he gave me, his face with a big smile at the pleasure he was getting in fucking my ass, a smile that I returned at having him where he was, deep inside and giving me that thrill of having his hard flesh moving inside me. He lasted a good ten minutes of reaming my ass before he held me tighter still and had his balls smacking my bum as he began to ram himself into me and had the thrill then of feeling his cum start to spray my insides. What joy and I gave out a cry of joy at feeling his cum start to fill me once again.

Both of us were breathing heavily when he'd finished cumming, my legs slipping off his shoulders and falling down by his side, the movement moving him back so that his cock slipped out to my cry of dismay. In spite of where his cock had just been, I couldn't help myself from turning round and taking his still hard cock head into my mouth, sucking out the remnants of his cum as well as tasting some of my own anal fluid at the same time.

He soon pushed me off from sucking on him for him to then take my throbbing cock into his mouth to suck and use his hand to bring about my orgasm, which wasn't long before I was bucking my hips up to him as I then gave him my cum that had been waiting to leave my body and enter his. What a relief it was to let go, for my cum had been boiling up in my balls from the moment he arrived, and now I went into a lethargic mode and just lay back as he kissed me all over my body, paying special attention to my small breasts and their nipples that he sucked and gently chewed on.

It was at least half an hour before I felt that his cock was hard enough to fuck me again, which I begged him to do and so he entered me again and fucked my brains out, giving me more of his cum that thrilled me no end.

But the time came for him to leave and it was with some regret that I kissed him goodbye with the promise that he would be back in town soon for us to suck and fuck.

***

SEVERAL DAYS later with me wanting another man, put an ad on Craigslist, making it quite clear that I wanted a man who wanted his dick sucked and for him to fuck me. I got quite a few messages from guys who wanted to do just that to me, giving me their phone numbers and a brief resume. One that I fancied lived in the next town which wasn't far away and so I called him and had a chat. It wasn't a problem me being in the next town and he agreed to come the next morning about nine and would give me a ring on arrival so that I could give him directions.

I gave the flat a good clean and I was up early next morning, all spruced up and on the dot of nine he phoned and said that he was in town and so gave him the address and within fifteen minutes he was at the door. He was a good looking man in his late twenties or early thirties, a shade under six foot and looked quite sturdy. But it was his eyes that drew my attention for they were the brightest blue I'd ever seen in a man as he smiled at seeing me saying his hello as I invited him in.

It was a bit early for beer so we had coffee and he asked if I had any good films on video and so I put on a porno one and sat down on the couch next to him. It was almost like a mirage image of us with two men sitting on a sofa and one started to stroke the trouser front of the other and so I did the same to Richard, for that was the name he had given me, truth or not, it didn't matter at me feeling what he had hidden from view but not from my stroking him. I guessed at what size he was and hoped that it looked as good as it felt as I undid the belt of his trousers and pulled down the zipper and put my hand inside.

It was hot in my hand and I pulled it out easily as he wasn't wearing any underpants and found that it was straight, hard and firm and about seven to eight inches long and fat enough at the base as I couldn't make my thumb and forefinger meet.

'This is a lovely cock you've got, Richard,' I said as I moved the soft silky skin up and down over the solid flesh beneath it as I slid off the couch and moved in between his open legs. 'It looks good enough to eat,' as I smiled up at him lying back with another smile on his face as I bent my head and took the head of his cock into my mouth. I pushed his foreskin down with my lips, feeling the bare flesh beneath me until I could get my tongue round the G-string, making him give out a groan.

I didn't want to suck on him too long for I now had an itch up inside my ass and wanted what I was sucking stuffed up inside me to scratch that itch.

'Boy, I'm gonna love this,' I said when I released him and rose up and gave him my hand and led him through to the bedroom where we both quickly got our clothes off for us both to look and admire each other's body with our rampant cocks sticking out in front of us. I passed him the lube as I got onto the bed and watched as he got quite a bit on his fingers and gave out a shiver when I felt a lubed finger work its way into my ass. He was gentle with his finger movements and I soon had two fingers in my ass for him to slowly widen my asshole to take his thick prick into me and with him satisfied that I was wide enough for his cock, lubed the head and got on the bed behind me as I much preferred being fucked in the doggie position because it was less strain on my back.

Oh, what bliss it was to have a cock once again probing at the entrance to my ass and have it slowly pushed in, widening me enough for the head to slip in and then have it pulsating inside me. He had paused with just the head in, letting me flex my muscle round it for a minute or two before he leaned in closer to me, making his cock slide in nice and easy till I had his thighs up against the cheeks of my bum with his whole cock throbbing away giving me all kinds of thrills at having him there inside me.

It was with a slow and steady moving of his hips that made his cock slide back and forth inside my ass, making me drool at the soothing massage I was being given with his hard cock.

'You've sure got one tight ass here, John,' he said as he moved himself in his fucking of me. 'I've not fucked an ass as tight as this before, it's just great, man.'

'Well, fuck me harder, Richard, for I want to feel your cum shoot into me,' I said, having had him fucking me now for nearly ten minutes and I now wanted that cum to coat my insides, to feel it come out of his cock to give that thrill when it splattered my channel. So he moved up a gear and began to ram himself into me, feeling his balls swing back and forth, slapping against my bum cheeks. This made my own hard cock bounce up and down and my balls swing the same as his, and I could feel my own cum starting to want its release from my balls.

His fingers were gripping my hips very tightly as he started to pull me back onto his forward thrusting cock and I loved the powerful feel of his cock reaming me as well as the solid smacking of his thighs up against my bum.

'I'm nearly there,' he grunted and a moment later, 'I'm cumming...I'm cumming,' and felt him stiffen up behind me as his first load of cum shot into me, spraying my insides with some force which made me drool at the pleasure of it. Not only did he shoot his cum into me for I shot mine out onto the bed without me even touching my cock. As he sprayed my asshole with his cum, I sprayed the bed with mine and looking down between my legs, I could see the streaming threads of my cum stretching from the eye of my cock to the mess I was making on the bed.

'Pure heaven, man,' I crooned. 'Pure heaven,' as he filled me, finishing off with one final thrust before coming to a stop and leaning over my rear end.

'That it is, man,' he panted, his hands now moving up my sides in a stroking action but using his fingernails to gently rake my flesh when he pulled them back. This made me shiver with delight at this action and begged for more as he then leaned fully on my back and used his fingers to nip the nipples on my small breasts, making them really stand out as hard little nuts. I groaned at all the different sensations that my body was feeling as his hard cock still throbbed inside me. The last act was to kiss the back of my neck before he straightened up and began to pull out of me, which was this part of having sex that I hated the most, losing that lovely fucking organ being taken away from me. But it was out and I flopped over onto my back, missing my mess on the bed and smiled up at him. His eyes shifted to see my hard cock still dripping my cum, lying on my stomach and he moved down onto his front and lifted it up and took the head into his mouth. He was hot and knew how to suck the rest of my cum out, making me tremble with delight as his tongue moved over the bare flesh that he'd uncovered.

With the head licked clean, he moved up my body and kissed me, letting me get a taste of my own cum in the process, our wilting cocks getting squashed between us. We didn't kiss for long and soon got up and he asked if he could have a shower before getting dressed. This was okay by me and I put my clothes on and went off to the kitchen to get some beers for it was now past coffee drinking time.

I passed him a can when he came out of the bedroom and he took it and sat down next to me on the couch. He popped it open and took a deep pull before looking at me with those lovely blue eyes.

'Well, John. I must say that that's the best session I've ever had,' he said as he patted my thigh.

'I think the pleasure was half mine,' I grinned back at him, stroking the front of his trousers. 'My! I think it's up ready again,' feeling that he was indeed getting hard inside his trousers. 'Mine too. Here, feel,' and I pulled his hand down to my lap and had another tremor run through me at his touch and I now rubbed his even more, wanting it again before he left.

Without asking, I got his zipper down and had his soft cock out and in my hand but it didn't stay soft for very long, for I was soon off the couch and had the whole thing in my mouth. It was lovely to suck and chew on and to feel it start to grow and slowly start to emerge from my mouth as it rose up to be one solid bar of flesh. He gave out a groan at my manipulation of not only his cock in my mouth but I also pulled his balls out of his trousers as I sucked on him, to fondle them with my fingers, moving them round in their sac.

In spite of it not being so long ago that he'd fucked me, he soon reached the point of no return and had his cum shoot out into my mouth. And what a load it was too, filling my mouth to capacity for me to hold it there till he'd finished cumming. I was thrilled to bits at getting that amount out of him in such a short time and found that my own cock was now really hurting such was its need for the same release. I fumbled my own erection out of my trousers and began to jerk myself off.

He had given out a groan at his release and with him opening his eyes, saw what I was doing to myself.

'No, John, no. Let me see to you the same way,' he said, his voice sounding rather throaty. So I stopped handling my own cock and giving his cock head a final suck and lick, I stood up, my cock sticking out in front of me. I moved back a little as he eased himself off the couch and going down onto his knees in front of me, his cock still hanging out of his trousers. He took the head and half the length of my cock into his hot mouth as his hands went round behind me to grasp the cheeks of my bum to pull me forward as he sucked and tongued me.

Just his handling of my butt made me get even harder and so put my hands to the sides of his head for me to take over and face fuck him. One of his hands came round to take hold of the lower end of my shaft so that I didn't push too far in to choke him as I really moved up into a full fucking mode. I could feel his teeth rasping the shaft as I moved my cock back and forth in his mouth and really held him tight as I started to cum. I didn't think that my balls could hold so much cum that erupted from my cock and I'm sure he had to swallow some of it or else choke.

I came to a full stop, feeling the sweat running down my chest and back at the effort I had put into that face fuck and waited till he gave the head a final lick and kiss before standing up. We went into each other's arms with our cocks clashing by still being outside of our trousers as he hugged and kissed each other in the pleasure we both had given and received.

We finally broke apart and put our wilting cocks away as I then saw him to the door where he thanked me for the best sex session he'd ever had. Whether it was the truth or not, it still pleased me for I had most certainly enjoyed the sex that we shared. So I was again left on my own.

But not for long for I went out and bought myself a poor substitute, that being a dildo. This I would lube up and shove up it my ass making believe it was the real thing which alas, it wasn't. The nearest I got to believing it was somewhere near that was that I found that if I put the base between the bed frame and the mattress, it was a just the right height to be level with my asshole. So with it lubed up, I would back myself onto it, feeling it expand my ring piece, taking it right in until the cheeks of my bum were up against the bed frame. I would then jerk myself off as I kept moving myself backwards and forwards having this dildo take the place of a man fucking me. So this became my means of being fucked and of me cumming at the same time, but as I've said, it was a poor thing compared to a real live throbbing cock, but it had to do.

***

IT WAS about two weeks later that I came across on the net, a married couple that wanted a male to join them in a threesome soon as they were only in town for the one night. I quickly made contact with them and after some chit chat between us, was invited round to where they were staying. It was a house of a friend of theirs who'd let them have it for the night while he was away, and it wasn't far from where I was now living. It was only going to be a one off session but I still had a good shower making sure my ass, cock and balls were really clean before drying myself and getting dressed. It was casual clothes, well two only, that being a light blue button shirt and a pair of light brown slacks that were rather tight in the leg so as to show what I had for I didn't put on any underpants. No socks on my feet but wore a pair of moccasins.

I walked to where they were staying, arriving at the time specified and was welcomed in, both husband and wife giving me a good look over and I think I passed their visual test. I'd noticed that both of them first studied my groin before their eyes covered the rest of my body and I also studied them. They were both about in their early thirties and she had lovely blue eyes and a wide smile that would take any sized cock. Brunette hair that shaped a lovely face and tits that were a perfect size for her five foot six body. He was taller by about five inches, dark hair and brown eyes and looked quite solidly built but couldn't really see what size he was in the cock department at this first look.

We introduced ourselves again, already having this ascertained on the web site, but this was the proper introduction, and shook hands first with Kelly, the wife, and then her husband Jim. I was taken into the lounge which couldn't be called a sitting room, being half again bigger than what was in my pad. Drinks were offered and I opted for beer, refusing the glass as did Jim though Kelly poured her beer into a glass.

It wasn't really small talk as such but more to the point of them telling me how they began to have threesomes whenever they could and had been doing this for five years of their eight years of marriage so far. Both were bi-sexual and I said that I only became bi-sexual about four years ago and was separated from my wife though I didn't go into the details of why.

While drinking her beer, Kelly had undone the buttons of the shirt she was wearing, letting me see her tits that were flashed as she did so with not wearing a bra. Knowing that I would probably be sucking them shortly, started to get a hard on inside my slacks. With the pant legs being fairly tight, it was obvious that I was getting an erection for it could clearly be seen down my left leg.

'Phew, it's warm in here,' she said after putting her empty glass down and flapping the lower halves of her shirt, letting my see those tits of hers again. 'Why don't we get these clothes off and get started. I can see that you are ready, John,' she said with a big grin on her face. 'So let's see if it's for real and not a dummy one you've got in your pants.'

She stood up and offered me her hand which I took as I got up from the sofa and let her lead me into the bedroom with Jim following behind. Behind was right, for I felt his hand stroke my bum as we left the lounge and knew what he wanted.

It was a big double bed they had there and Kelly was the first to strip off, showing her shaved pussy to me as she got onto the bed and laid down, her hands running over her tits and smiled at me. My few clothes were off next and they could both then see that I sported a seven-inch throbbing cock that stuck out from my thighs and I managed not to gasp when I saw that Jim's cock must have been at least ten inches in length and as wide as a beer can when I saw it sticking out right in front of him. I don't know where he got the strength from to not have it droop down with it being that size.

Kelly patted the bed and waved her hand at me and so I got on next to her.

'I want to suck on that cock of yours while Jim fucks me so I can be filled with cum at both ends,' she said. So I moved up onto my knees near her head and waited for Jim who was just getting onto the bed and between her open legs. His massive cock swayed about as he got into position and I watched him slide that enormous cock up into his wife's cunt. 'Oooh, lovely,' she crooned when he was fully inside her and could imagine him flexing it. 'Now your cock, John,' and opened that wide mouth and easily took the head in as I leaned over her face.

Boy, she really knew how to suck cock in that position though she held the base of it so that I wouldn't choke her. Her mouth was hot and her teeth sharp as they raked across the bare flesh of the head, her tongue working its magic on my G-string, making me shiver with the erotic sensations it caused. As she sucked on me, I had Jim's head almost butting me as he fucked her, grunting away as he pushed his ten-inch length in her making her give out strange sounds round my cock.

Kelly pulled her head away from my cock to give out a gasp. 'I'm nearly there, Jim, nearly there. Fuck me harder!' she cried before taking my cock back inside her mouth. She was almost chewing on me as she approached her orgasm, Jim's head now butting my waist as he moved up a gear in his fucking of her, panting heavily and looking back, saw his body tauten as he lifted his head.

'I'm cumming......I'm cumming,' he cried as just his hips moved now with him up on straightened arms. 'Aaaaah,' he sighed as his first salvo exploded inside her and her mouth tightened on me as she was now beginning to squirm under me and I let loose my cum, shooting it straight down her throat.

Kelly and I were in frenzied movements while Jim was only pumping his hips, sending out charge after charge of his cum into her while she was bucking about in her orgasm, almost gnawing me to bits and me striving to keep my pulsating cock in position that was spewing out my cum into her mouth. This action, feverish as it was, only lasted a few moments, thank heavens, before we all seemed to calm down. Kelly now swallowing what cum she had from my cock and I expected she was squeezing Jim's cock that was still inside her.

I pulled out and rolled over onto my back, flexing my arms from their stiffness of supporting my upper body from squashing her face. I watched Jim start to move back to see his shiny wet cock emerge from her pussy, still as big as before and moving up and down to the pulse beat of the blood moving around to keep it erect.

'John! Eat my pussy while I suck Jim's cock,' she said, though it sounded like an order to me, and did as I was told as Jim moved up on one side of her as I moved down on the other. I saw him straddle her with his back towards me and had the sudden urge to goose him with his ass right there in front of me, but refrained for he might have driven his cock right down her throat and killed her. I looked at the hairless pudenda and licked all over the labia before moving in closer to stick my tongue up into her wet pussy. I was then getting two for the price of one. Her orgasmic juices as well as cum from Jim and I loved the mixed taste of the pair of them and sucked away and there endeth the first of our encounters as a threesome.

***

WE HAD a break, Jim going off to the kitchen to come back with some more beers which we greedily drank while trying to get our strength back, which really didn't take that long considering we had emptied our balls of our cum. Them having started immediately after dispatching the first growth, were quickly producing more for our pleasure.

'Scene two,' said Jim looking at me from over Kelly's bared tits. 'I want to fuck you while you're fucking Kelly. Is that alright with you?' he asked of me.

'Fine by me,' I said, 'But with one provision.'

'What's that?' he asked.

'You take it easy with the entry. I've not had a cock the size of yours before so I don't want it ripping me apart,' I said.

'That's no problem. I've had that said before, so I'll lube you up first and make sure that you're wide enough to take me in,' he said with a smile. I think my smile back was rather a bit on the sickly side not knowing if he was telling the truth or not. But I followed his instructions when we were both ready and rampant again, me swallowing hard at seeing what I was going to have shoved up my ass in a minute or two.

'You'll enjoy this, I promise you,' Kelly said to me with a smile as I got between her legs in the doggie fashion, on my knees and supporting my upper body on my outstretched arms. I had seen Jim get the lube and now felt one such covered finger enter the hole of my ass. I flinched at the first touch but relaxed with the smooth moving of his finger up in my ass. That was easy enough to take with it moving about for a minute or so to then be withdrawn and then have two fingers pushed into me. It was when four fingers were being used that it was uncomfortable, but after a few minutes of him working them round in my asshole, it wasn't so bad, but by then Kelly was getting rather fidgety.

'Enough, Jim, enough. Kelly is starting to steam, so get that prick of yours inside me so that I can see to Kelly as you see to me,' I said, and gritted my teeth after the fingers had been pulled out knowing that I was now going to get a cock the size that I'd never had before. I couldn't help but flinch at the first touch of his cock to the entrance to my cave, but thanked the lube for the pain wasn't as bad as I thought it would be because of his earlier finger movements to widen me to be able to take the thickness of his cock into my ass.

But the head was inside and throbbing away as he paused for a moment as I flexed my inner muscle around the girth of his cock before he pushed in a little bit more, then more and then even more until I had the whole ten inches up in my ass and I let out an explosion of breath that I'd been holding. You did it, my mind cried out. You've now got the biggest cock so far up your ass, so enjoy the fucking you're now going to get.

With him buried deep within me, creating all kinds of new sensations at having a cock reach parts that no other had done before, I clamped my muscle round it as hard as I could as I slowly eased myself forward, bringing him down with me. My own cock was now one solid mass of muscle that was throbbing away like crazy as I felt the head start to slide up into Kelly's pussy. She was the one who had to bear the weight of two of us on her pubes as I came down to rest on my elbows either side of Kelly's gorgeous tits, to have Jim's hands support him by being at full stretch either side of my arms.

I was in and throbbing away inside Kelly as Jim was inside me, doing exactly the same, pulsating like crazy now that he was up into the depths of my ass, and it was now up to him to start the ball rolling. Well, the fucking anyway.

He pulled back out of me, this was a thrill on its own, before he then pushed forward making me move into Kelly more and with my body acting like a coiled spring, when he pulled back out of me, I moved back and pulled back from Kelly. So with his steady back and forth movements, I was doing the same to Kelly's pussy.

What a glorious fuck! With him fucking me and me fucking her, his wife, and I loved it. Feeling him throbbing away inside me as I did the same to her, having her inner muscles flexing themselves round my cock as I shafted her, my muscles doing the same to that wonderful fucking organ that was now reaming my back passage. What bliss! It was a strenuous effort on my part to hold my cumming back for I had wanted to let go the moment I entered her. His balls were like a pendulum, swinging down to knock mine to swing the same to hit the cheeks of her ass, really agitating the sperm in mine that I was holding back until he came. Boy, did he have some staying power or not! It was a good five minutes of him reaming me with that lovely big cock before he began to grunt and start to really pound my ass making me do the same to Kelly beneath me.

'I'm nearly there, Jim,' she cried out for which I was thankful and leaned into her and kissed her. She smiled back up at me, her hands now on my shoulders and I could feel her finger nails really digging into my shoulders as she began to buck beneath me.

'I can't hold out much longer, Jim,' I cried out, my cock now really being rammed into Kelly's cunt.

'I'm......I'm......Aaaaah,' he groaned and I felt the head of his cock swell a little more and felt that first shot of his cum hit my insides. Boy, didn't I then let go of my first salvo into Kelly. She gave out a scream as she began her orgasm and I felt it coming down to coat my cock as I sent more of my cum up into her as more of Jim's cum came spurting into me.

I could see the sweat on Kelly's forehead and knew that I was in the same state as I saw drops fall onto her body and I'm sure that Jim was sweating too at the effort he was putting into the fucking of me. How we managed to stay up and not fall onto Kelly's body I don't know as we came to a stop, panting hard as though we'd just run a record mile. My chest was heaving as was that of Kelly, her tits rising up for me to feel the rock hard nipples crush themselves to my chest and imagined that Jim was doing the same in the expanding of his chest.

'Wow!' Kelly breathed out. 'That was some fuck!'

'You can say that again,' I panted.

'Wow! That was some fuck!' and grinned up at me and felt her vaginal muscles flex themselves round my still pulsating cock inside her. I grinned back at her and then grimaced as I felt that lovely fucking tool of Jim start to be pulled out of my ass.

'Oh, Jim,' I cried, it almost being a sob as I felt it slide out of me and then feel the cool air move round my asshole as it began to revert to its normal state. This part of having a fuck was the worse at having that cock removed from your asshole, that had just made you feel so much alive with its moving and eventual cumming inside. With his weight up off of my own back, I was able to then pull out of Kelly, much to the same cry that I had given out.

Jim had rolled over onto his back on one side of Kelly and I rolled onto the other side, still breathing hard.

'Cock sucking time,' I heard Kelly cry out and had her moving between us. If fact we all moved about so that it became a three way suck. It was awkward, but we managed it, me not having any compunction about taking Jim's still hard cock into my mouth as Kelly was on the end of mine like a limpet to suck away. Jim was now between her legs licking and sucking at her pussy and so that's how we finished up the three-way fuck and the cleaning in the aftermath.

***

'I THOUGHT you were going to kill me with that truncheon of yours,' I said to Jim as we drank another beer after we had finished the second session and guessed that this next one would be me fucking Jim, which is what happened.

They waited until I was up and ready before Kelly laid herself out on the bed with her legs open for Jim to get in between them on his knees to start eating and sucking on her pussy. Lubed up, I got between Jim's legs and opened up the crease of his bum cheeks and pushed my erection into his asshole. He was hot and tight but had no trouble in taking my cock inside in one movement. He had grunted as he snuffled in her wet pussy, slurping away at her juices as I moved back and forth in my fucking of him. It was just perfect and I came with some gusto, shooting my cum up his ass to little cries of pleasure from him as I did so.

When I'd finished, Kelly told me to go and wash myself as she wanted to suck on me while Jim fucked me for the second time. This I did and saw that he was up and ready for me when I returned and got back onto the bed. I went onto my hands and knees as he got behind me and Kelly waited till I had Jim fully inside me. It had taken a few minutes for him to ease his massive cock inside me and I positively glowed at having that huge cock pulsating away inside me again.

As he started to fuck me in a glorious fashion, Kelly slithered beneath me and had her take my balls into her mouth first and had obviously told Jim to take it steady at the beginning of fucking me so that she wouldn't tear my balls from my body with any violent movement on his part. It was lovely to have his prick sliding in and out of me as she manipulated my balls in their sac until she then started to nibble at the underside of my now fully erect cock that had risen with the pleasure of both being sucked and fucked.

This third session lasted nearly twenty minutes and I simply loved it at having his cock ream for that length of time before having his cum shoot up my ass, filling me not only with his cum, but delight too.

***

WE HAD one more session and that was Jim lying on his back with Kelly kneeling over him in the sixty-nine position so that she could be plated by him while she sucked on his cock. This gave me a choice of whether to fuck her pussy in this position or fuck her up the ass. So I did both.

I went up into her wet cunt first, moving nice and smoothly inside her cavern, for that's what it felt like, big and plenty of space for my cock to easily move, feeling her flex her muscles in the process. But this really was only to get enough lubrication on my cock before I changed venues.

In my fucking of her pussy, I would push in deep and then slowly bring my cock right out before plunging back inside her, getting used to me pulling out until when I thought my cock was lubricated enough, pulled out and unerring hit the target of her asshole and rammed myself right in to her giving out a big gasp at my entry. I don't think she had any pain because her body was relaxed and didn't have time to bring her sphincter muscle into play, well until I was fully inside her ass. Boy, she was tight, which made me think that she either hadn't had Jim's cock up her ass or she didn't have it very often. But a fuck is a fuck whichever hole was used and I enjoyed this fucking of a new asshole.

I don't know whether Jim gave her any of his cum as she sucked on him but she certainly got mine, and it made her give out a little cry when my first load of cum hit her insides and had her muscle now really squeezing me hard as I jerked away at her rear, giving her the rest of the cum that my balls had produced.

She told me afterwards that it had only been the second time that she'd had a cock up her ass and now would like to have it more often, but sadly, she said, not with me for they would be leaving town the next day. So with us now dressed, I got to kiss both from them and thanked for giving them the pleasure of my company for the day.

Chapter Nine

After three weeks of non-male sex, or female if it comes to that, I went onto Craigslist and ran across a post from a guy looking for fun with another guy. It had only been put on the list that day, so I replied to this post and got an e-mail back almost at once. It was from a guy named James, and he said that he was on his way to town and so I gave him my phone number to let me know when he arrived.

It was about seven o'clock when he rang and I gave him my address and within half an hour he was at my door. He was in his early forties, and well-built and I joked that he looked like a quarter back, which it turned out he had been when in his late teens. He stood at six feet, so his eye level was just above mine and he had a nice smile and took to him immediately.

He accepted a beer and we sat in the sitting room for a quick chat before we got down to the reason of him being here with me.

'Are you a top or bottom man, James?' I asked him.

'I like sex both ways,' he chuckled, giving his crotch a rub and I noticed that he already had an erection there.

'So do I,' I said, rubbing myself and clearly outlining that I too was already sporting an erection at the thought of having male sex after three weeks of abstinence, thinking then of a quote I once read, "Absence might make the heart grow fonder, but abstinence doesn't make sex last longer." It was from "College Teacher" I think. 'So let's go into where the bed is,' and led him through where we both took our clothes off. He had developed a slight paunch but it was his cock that I really looked at and saw that he must be about the same size as me of being seven inches when fully erect. We both started to speak at the same time and laughed.

'You first, John,' he said.

'What I was going to say was that I think you got a lovely looking cock there.'

'Funny,' he laughed. 'That was the very words I was going to say about yours,' and we went into a hug to kiss, making our two cocks make friends with each other as they got squashed up between us. 'I can't stay long, John, for I've got to be at work at six tomorrow morning.'

'Okay, let's get started then,' I said, giving his cock a stroke. We got onto the bed in the sixty-nine position and had his lovely cock right in front of me and greedily took the head into my mouth. It was throbbing nicely as I pushed the foreskin down to gently chew on the bare flesh and excite the G-string with my tongue. It was grand to have such a cock back in my mouth again and thoroughly enjoyed the sucking of it. I played with his balls with my left hand as I used the right to work the skin of his shaft up and down. It was a pleasure to be doing this and having the same done to me at the same time.

'I'm not far off cumming,' James said, taking his head up off my cock briefly before going back down on me.

'Okay,' I mumbled round his cock, and held him tighter as I worked on his cock and felt the head swell a little and actually felt his cum moving up inside his cock and had it shoot into my mouth. What bliss! To have a man's cum in my mouth again to savour the taste, each man having a different flavour to their cum was heaven for me. More cum shot into my mouth to join up until he came to a stop and I was then able to swill it all round the head before swallowing it.

I felt the extra suction on my cock and knew that he had just swallowed my cum as I began to lick the head of his cock clean before easing the foreskin back up to partly cover the exposed head and gave the eye a kiss before letting it go and waited for James to finish licking mine.

'That was grand,' James said after I had turned round to face him, to kiss and stroke him.

'Not only do our cocks look alike, I think we think alike too, for that's almost the same as what I was going to say,' and we both laughed before our mouths met to kiss and tongue each other. This we did along with our stroking of each other as well as fondling each other's balls and cock to make it rise up again for us to fuck each other. This took nearly half an hour before we were both sporting rigid cocks that were then ready for use.

'Fuck me first, John, and then my cock will be even harder for you,' he said, and so I lubed up my erection and put some on my fingers and worked them inside his anus as he knelt on the bed until his hole felt ready for my cock to be shoved in there.

What pleasure it was to once again look down and see the head of my cock slowly disappear into another man's ass to feel the pressure around it as I pushed myself into the heated insides and feel the muscle there constantly gripping the shaft as the rest of my cock slipped in. It was great to have my cock smoothly move in and out, giving us both the pleasure in doing so though it didn't last long and I was soon holding his hips firmly, pulling him back onto me as I began ramming myself hard into him. My thighs mashing up to the cheeks of his bum as my balls smacked against them at the same time and then going rigid myself as just my hips jerked as I sent my cum straight up into his ass.

'Wow, John! I felt every shot,' James gasped as I came to a halt.

'Well, I hope you give me as much,' I panted and pulled out to let him move round behind me to give me what I had been wanting ever since our first contact. I felt his knees touch my legs as he got into position and just having his hands part the cheeks of my bum I got that shiver of delight and also when I felt his lubed cock head touch the entrance to my portal. Wow, it was just great to once again have a cock widen me and slip inside, feeling it throb and then pulsate when the whole length was inside and he could go no further.

Back and forth he moved, making me drool at the internal massage I was getting as he smoothly slid about inside me, setting all my nerves atingle. But the pleasure of having a cock up my ass is a short lived one and he was soon holding my hips tight as he jerked away, sending his cum into me, coating my back passage as I felt every shot and was sent skywards at the thrill of feeling it splatter my insides before he came to a full stop, leaning over my back as he panted for breath.

'Fucking wonderful,' I grunted and then gave out a small cry as I felt his hard cock start to pull out, squeezing it as hard as I could to try and hold him there, but to no avail and felt myself widen slightly as the head left my ass. 'I just wish that you could have lasted longer, James. It was so nice having you fuck me.'

'I wish I could too, but when it wants to let go, there's nothing I can do about it,' he said, giving my bum a gentle slap. 'But I've got to go as I've got to be up at six for work in the morning.'

So we got off the bed and went and had a shower together, soaping and washing the cock of each other to clean off any lube and residue of our cumming. Dried and dressed, we kissed each other and he promised to come to town as soon as he could and so with one final kiss, he left.

***

IT WAS a couple of weeks before I got an e-mail from him asking if it was alright to come over the next evening to which I quickly sent back a reply saying that I would like it. Another came back saying that he would be with me about six-thirty, so I cleaned up the flat a little and prepared something for us to eat and was ready when he turned up.

My heart gave a bounce at the knocking at the front door and knew that it was my lovely fucker and quickly let him in for us to once again have a kiss and a hug before we went into the sitting room. I gave him a beer and put a porn DVD on the television as I went and got our meal out onto trays and we sat and ate as we watched two men suck and fuck each other on the screen.

Our meal was soon finished and after taking the trays back to the kitchen, I returned to find that he'd already taken his clothes off and was standing there naked with his cock up and rigid and nearly creamed myself at seeing it there waiting for me to suck on it. I quickly got my things off and showed that I was up and hard too as I pushed him back down onto the couch, his cock bouncing up and down that made me start to drool at the mouth.

'I want to try and deep throat you,' I said as I got down between his legs, 'so don't push up but let me take it easy for I've not done this before.' He smiled down at me kneeling there as I held his cock still and ran a hand through my hair as I bent my head and took the head of his cock into my mouth.

What bliss to have his throbbing cock head there again and slowly eased as much saliva out to make the shaft easier to take in and slowly eased it into my mouth and touch the back of my throat. I tried not to gag as it did so and it took a few minutes to be able to open my gullet and get the head into my throat until I had my nose buried in his pubic hairs. I could now really get a smell of his body odour which was like perfume to me as I slowly moved my head up and down, feeling his cock slide up and down at the entrance to my throat.

'Wow!' he gasped. He loved that word. 'Wow' he said again. 'I've never had my cock that far in a mouth before. It's great and I'm about to cum.'

I couldn't say anything with his cock stuck in there and could only give his thighs a squeeze as I began to move my head a little faster and it wasn't long before I had his cum start shooting it straight down my throat. It was then that I realised that I wasn't getting to taste him this way and so I eased back so that I could have the rest of his cum come into my mouth for me to savour the taste before swallowing it. It took some effort to lift my head up off of him for I just loved having his cock in my mouth, but I did and licked the head clean and gave it a kiss before getting up and sitting down on the couch next to him.

'That was lovely, James,' I said with a smile, giving his cock, which was still quite hard, another stroke. 'My turn now,' and had him give mine a stroke before he got off the couch and in between my legs.

I gave out a big sigh and leaned my head back as I had his hot mouth take the head of my cock into it and begin sucking on me. I was good and because I was so wound up, soon gave him the cum that had been at boiling point for some time inside my balls. It was good and I wondered who was the better cocksucker between us, but it would take a third party to be able to say which of us was the better.

We rested for a little while for us to rise up again and had him lube his fingers and work them inside my ass, widening me up for our fucking session. He also lubed his cock and when it looked hard enough, I got up and then sat back down onto his lap, having his now rampant cock sliding quite easily into my ass without any pain at all at the entry. It was nice having his hard cock throbbing away inside me as I gently bounced up and down on him.

'Let's do it properly,' he said, lifting me up off of him and pushed me down onto the carpet where I landed on my knees and had him then get behind me and shove his cock back into my ass. This was just as good but he now had control of how he fucked me which was what he wanted and took his time in the fucking of me. 'You really like having a hard cock up in your ass, don't you?' he asked as he moved himself back and forth, giving me a lovely internal massage. To which I had to say yes for it was the truth, I did like a hard cock fuck me, big, small, large or little were all the same in the pleasure that they gave me. 'I can't stay long because of work tomorrow,' he said, which is what he had said the last time he was with me.

'Well, if we haven't the time for me to fuck you,' I grunted, 'jerk me off while you're inside me so that I can get rid of my cum as you give me yours.'

So as he kept moving himself inside me, his hand came down and took of my now hard cock and began working on it. This was just as good as fucking him, having him fuck me while jerking me off. With him half on my back, ramming himself into me as he worked on my cock, I felt my sap rising.

'I'm nearly there,' I gasped, and had the thrill of feeling his cock harden some more and had his cum shoot out into my ass. That was when I let go, and having bent my head down, I saw it all shoot out to land on the carpet as his filled my ass. It was great watching my cum in its stream, making a puddle beneath me and had the last strings of it still hanging out of the eye when I'd finished.

I gave out a groan as he pulled out and I lifted myself up and looked down at my dripping cock and wished that I was double jointed for I could then have bent right down and sucked on my own cock to get the last drops. As I couldn't, all I could do was take those last drops onto my fingers and suck my cum off that way. It still tasted nice and a bit better than his, I thought as I swallowed these last remnants of my cum.

We went and had a shower, both washing each other until we were clean of lube, cum and sweat before drying and getting dressed. Well, James getting dressed for I stayed naked and then we kissed as we said our goodbyes and I was once again alone. Though thinking of the past couple of hours, I sat and watched the porn movie again and when I was up and hard, jerked myself off, catching my cum in my hand to then suck it all up to swallow, making believe that it was the cum of James.

***

I GOT an e-mail from Charles a couple of days later saying that he would be in town on the Friday and he duly turned up in the afternoon and it wasn't long before we were both naked, kissing and playing with our hard cocks. His need was greater than mine I think for in a very short time, I was bent over the arm of the couch and had his lovely cock reaming my ass and cumming inside to my great pleasure at having him and his cum where it was.

We then went into the bedroom for him to have a wash while I got onto the bed and had him come out and immediately go down on me, almost doing a deep throat as he sucked on my cock, teasing the G-string and gently chewing on the bare flesh of the head before making me cum in his mouth. I felt the extra suction as he swallowed it and continued to suck and then lick all around the head before giving the eye of my cock a kiss before raising his head with a big smile.

He rose up onto his knees and I saw that just with his sucking on me made his cock rise up to be a rampant tool that seemed to pulsate as he shuffled up between my legs and lifted them up to his shoulders. I had the lube to hand and passed it to him for him to then coat his fingers and have two and then three inserted into my asshole, widening me for his cock which was swaying about as his fingers touched my prostate and made me quiver in anticipation of what I was going to get in a moment or two. He then pulled his fingers out from their fucking of me to lube his cock before tossing the tube to me as he held my thighs tight to his chest as he started to double me up as he leaned forward and had the thrill of feeling the head of his cock start to enter me.

Already being widened, his head slipped in for me to feel it throb as he paused and shuffled that little bit closer till his lower thighs were tight up to the cheeks of my arse before plunging right in till I felt his balls smack against my bum. Wow, it was great to have him fill me for my muscle to flex itself round his shaft and have him pulsating inside me. We both smiled at each other as he began to move in his fucking of my ass. What joy! What heaven to have his lovely big cock reaming my back passage again and crooned as he fucked, making my own cock bounce up and down on my stomach.

My legs slipped off his shoulders and he freed his arms for my legs to move round and clamp themselves round his waist to help me pull him harder into me as his hands came down to lift my bum up a bit more so that he had a straighter entry as he continued to plough my field of dreams. In spite of me having cum a few minutes ago, more began to squirt out of my cock to splash on my lower chest as he kept on grinding himself into my ass until he stiffened up and felt the head of his cock swell some more and he began to shoot his cum into my ass.

I crooned and drooled as I felt his seed coating my canal as more and more kept hitting me, adding more lubrication to make his cock slide even smoother as he moved it back and forth now that he had cum. He kept up his fucking of me even though he'd finished cumming and only slowed down as his cock started to slowly wilt before he then pulled out, making me give out a little cry at this loss of having his throbbing organ that pleasured me.

So this ended our session of sex for the night with us getting off the bed and going to the bathroom for a shower and I just loved the feel of having his cum slowly easing itself out of my ass and starting to slide down my inner thighs as I walked into the bathroom with our arms holding each other. We showered together, soaping each other in turn, making sure that our cocks and my ass were clean of both cum and lube before moving out to dry ourselves.

It was with sorrow as I watched that lovely cock of his disappear as he pulled up his pants as we got dressed and then it was a hug and kiss as we said our goodbye and he left, promising to come again next time he was in town.

***

A FEW days later I had Bobby, another man that had fucked and sucked me, phone to ask if it was alright to come round to which the answer was a resounding yes, him with his eight-inch cock was welcome anytime to enter my home and me in that order. So making sure that both the flat, bedroom and myself were clean, I was ready and waiting for him to call. Eventually there was a knock at the door and I got a big surprise when I opened it to find my old friend Bruce standing there.

'Well, fuck me, Bruce!' I cried, flinging myself into his arms and giving him a kiss before pulling him inside and closing the door. 'Where did you spring from? How did you know where I'm now living?'

'It took a little while but I found out where you were and as I had to come to town decided to drop in and see my old friend again,' he smiled and I rubbed my hand down the front of his trousers and felt that he was semi hard there and smiled back at him.

'Which one?' I smiled back at him as I took his hand and rubbed my crotch for him to feel that I had a hard on. 'This, or me?' and had him laugh.

'Well, both if it comes to that.'

'Cum is what I want,' I said, making a pun of the word as I guided him into the sitting room and made him sit down on the couch while I got us a beer each. We drank and talked for a bit before I started to fondle his front and finally slipped off the couch and undid the front of his trousers and pulled out his now hard and upright cock.

'What a pleasure to feel and see you again,' I said to his cock before I bent down and gave the half exposed head of his cock a kiss, tonguing the eye as well to make his body give out a shiver. I then took the whole length of his cock into my mouth, pushing the foreskin back as I did so for me to be able to really work my tongue on that erogenous piece of flesh that joined it to the head. I could feel the tremor he gave out vibrate through his thighs that I was leaning on and I really loved chewing on his cock and wished he had come round earlier.

He gave out a groan as I managed to deep throat him, having my nose buried in his pubic hair which tickled my nose, getting the full smell of him not having been able to do this to him before. I really worked my mouth and tongue on his cock, giving him my best so that he would visit me again for more of this sucking of his cock and it wasn't long before I felt him stiffening up and had him give me his cum that shot out of the eye of his cock. It was lovely to once again have the taste of him in my mouth, to move it round the bare flesh of the head, savouring it before having that extra thrill as I swallowed and had it sliding down my throat. I almost choked as that little song sang in my head, 'round the mouth, teeth and gums, look out stomach, here it cums.'

I was just licking and cleaning the head of his cock when there was a knocking at the door.

'Who's that!' Bruce said in an alarmed voice, sitting up on the couch making his cock slip out of my mouth.

'Shit!' I exclaimed. 'It's Bobby come round for a session with me,' I said as I used his thighs to lever myself up from between his legs. 'Won't be a mo',' I said as I went off to let Bobby in. We went back into the sitting room where I found Bruce was now standing up, his cock away back inside his trousers.

'Well I'd better be off for my appointment,' he said, giving me a kiss and quickly left the flat. I didn't get a chance to tell him to come again as soon as he liked, for I had missed out on not having him suck on me as well as getting him to fuck me.

'Who was that?' Bobby asked, now giving me a kiss.

'An old and dear friend,' I said. 'We were at school together.'

'And an old lover,' he added.

'Yes, but not as good as you,' I lied, moving into him for us to kiss and have our tongues talk to each other. 'God, I need this,' I said, rubbing the front of his trousers to feel that he was hard and ready for me.

'So do I, John. Blow me first,' he said, and so I pushed him down to where Bruce had sat and did the same to him as I did to Bruce, getting his lovely cock out and sucked, licked and deep throated him for him to finally cum for my second load to taste and swallow only this time, I had my cock sucked and gave up the cum that had really built up in my balls. 'Lovely as ever,' he said, licking his lips after swallowing my cum. 'I also want some of it inside my ass.'

'So do I, Bobby, so let's go to bed,' and led him into the bedroom where we undressed and when naked, got onto the bed to kiss and fondle each other until we were both fully aroused again.

Boy did we fuck! We fucked each other three times that evening and he even slept over and so we had another fuck in the morning before he left, leaving me well satisfied at having him a total of four times in our coupling as well as sucking on his cock in between.

I was now getting so many men wanting to come and fuck me and give me their cum that I had to get a diary and put their names down and give out dates that I was available for them to be sucked and fuck me. I was living the life that I now wanted, to suck and be fucked for I like being with other men.

THE END

Here is a sample from another story you may enjoy:

The Square Circle

MURDER IS THE NAME
OF THE GAME

SEDUCTIVE SUSPENSE

Amy Redek

The cafeteria, as expected, was crowded. The queue wasn't as long as Francis thought as she picked up her tray and joined the end of it. Francis Mann didn't mind the bustle of the city, coming from the small town of Malden in Essex. She had driven into Chelmsford with her husband, and they had travelled down by train that morning to London. Him to go to work while she went on this shopping expedition. Francis was just past her thirty-ninth birthday, dreading the next one, but was happy that she could still pass for a late twenty-year-old. Her figure, while not exactly hourglass, was still trim in spite of giving birth to a daughter twenty years previously. Her bust was nice and matronly and her legs were still slender that finished down at size five shoes. Ash blonde hair that didn't seem to need brushing at any time, framed a face once described as beautiful but now called very pretty. The pencilled eyebrows above soft brown eyes that had only a hint of mascara so as not to be distractive, led down to a short, but straight nose above her soft lips.

Behind her in the queue stood Penelope Swithers, though she always preferred to be known as Penny. She was only out that day because she was bored at home. Home being a house in Knightsbridge, so she hadn't travelled very far to be in the store. Penny was thirty years old and looked like a model in her trim suit having the figure that you would never see on a catwalk. Top heavy was her own description of herself, but from there down, perfect. She too was blonde, but tending more to the brunette colour than that of Francis before her in the queue. Her face was long but balanced by the wide blue eyes and generous mouth separated by her nose that on a round-faced person would have been large, but suited her perfectly.

Francis reached the till and paid for her tea, pastry and small chocolate bar, and moved off. Penny paid for her coffee, a slice of cake and a peach, and followed on through the crowded tables and nearly lost the lot when Francis suddenly stopped to turn round.

'Oh sorry,' said Francis, seeing the tray Penny was carrying, nearly tilt the contents off. 'I didn't realise anyone was behind me. This place is so full I can't see an empty seat.'

'There's an empty table over there,' Penny said, indicating with her chin across the shoulder of Francis.

'Oh you're right,' she replied after looking round, 'let's grab it quick before anyone else.'

They moved quickly between the other full tables, neatly swerving around crooked elbows and side stepping the bags and parcels that were in every little aisle. The table was in a corner and had just been vacated, but was still littered with trays and used crockery and other debris.

'Here, hold my tray a moment,' Penny said, handing her tray to Francis as they reached the table. 'I'll clear this off for us.'

Francis stood with both trays in her hands while Penny scooped all the litter onto two of the trays and looking round, but not finding anywhere they could go, gave a grin to Francis and pushed them between the two long flower troughs that bordered the eating area.

'Let them pick those up later,' she smiled, taking her tray back and sitting down. Francis pulled out a chair and setting her tray on the table, sat down opposite.

Two other women saw the table being cleared and both made a beeline for the two vacant seats that were there. The first was Anne Seymour, and apart from her hair being a soft brown, could have been the bookend for Penny, her figure being almost the same. She was big breasted above a trim waist and had long slim legs with well-rounded calves, and like Penny, was only thirty years old.

'May I join you?' she asked of Francis and Penny, standing by the table.

'By all means,' Francis replied with a slight wave of the hand, and Anne put her tray down and sat next to her.

'Can I too?' asked Jane, eyeing the last seat and having heard Anne ask the question.

'Certainly,' said Penny, removing her handbag from the last chair. With a sigh, Jane gratefully sank down on the seat beside her.

'Hi! I'm so glad to get off my feet. My name's Jane. Short for Jane,' she said with a little laugh. 'Yours?' was the query left in the air.

'Anne.'

'Francis.'

'Penny.'

'Well it's nice to meet you. I've just had a bellyful of this place. Worse than Epsom on Derby day. Bet you've never seen a crowd like this before in here?' Jane was married to a book-maker, hence her manner of speech and outgoing personality. London born and bred, she oozed the very spirit of a person raised within the sounds of Bow Bells. Short sharp pithy words and quick head movements like a pigeon constantly looking out for signs of danger. Shorter than the others, but not by much.

Again, thirty years old, but with her round face framed by her black hair at shoulder length, looked younger, except for the little lines at the corner of the eyes that only another woman would see to guess her age correctly. Her figure was slimmer than the others' and not quite in proportion having smaller breasts, thicker waist and fuller hips. Too much eating in restaurants or from hot dog stands at racetracks was not a healthy way to eat.

'It is a trifle crowded,' Anne admitted, sipping her tea, 'I only came to get out of the house for a while.'

'Me too. All day cooped up, never seeing anyone gets you really depressed,' replied Penny.

'I can spend all day in the garden and still not see a soul go past,' chipped in Francis.

'Where do you live then?' asked Penny.

'Just outside the village of Malden, in Essex,' she replied.

'An Essex girl!' sniggered Jane.

'Not at all,' Francis replied indignantly, 'I was born in Sussex. My husband was born in Essex though.'

'Do the old jokes apply to them too?' enquired Penny with a straight face, but a hint of a smile at her lips.

'I think so,' was the laughing reply, 'boring, and as much sex appeal as a lamppost,' nibbling on her pastry.

'That's the trouble with my husband. Too much sex appeal. I never see the bastard much these days,' said Penny gloomily, looking down into her empty cup. 'I wish one of his popsie's would take him off my hands. The divorce settlement would suit me down to the ground.'

'Well I see mine too much. I'm dragged from racecourse to racecourse. But then, when I don't go, I hear he has some tart with him. Yes, a divorce settlement would sort me out too!' Jane put in.

'Humph,' snorted Anne, 'if my husband saw another woman, he wouldn't know what to do. He wouldn't have the time anyway. You can set your watch by his habits. Divorce would be no good to me, he's worth more with his life insurance.'

Pushing her empty plate a little and dabbing at her lips with a tissue, Francis said, 'I'm in the same boat there, though I'm worth more dead to him than he is to me. Must sort that out one day, then maybe it would be worthwhile having him bumped off!' She gave a little hiccup. 'Oh do excuse me,' she said with a little laugh.

'I wish someone would do that for me,' Penny said wistfully.

'Kill him you mean?' asked Jane.

'Why not? He might just as well be dead for what I see of him. Besides, I wouldn't waste money like he does.'

'I don't get any money, well not much to speak of. For this shopping trip I have to use a credit card with a limit given me by my husband!' said Anne.

'That *is* the limit,' declared Jane, and then in a musing tone, 'I could take over the bookmaking and keep all the money myself. Or take in a partner. Perhaps you, Penny. Instead of his slogan, "A pound for a Pound," we could make it "In for a Penny, in for a Pound."' She laughed gaily, and the others did too.

'What about you, Anne?' asked Penny, 'No credit card limit. The sky would be the limit.'

'I don't know,' she said, absently stirring her spoon round in an empty cup before realising what she was doing, letting the spoon drop clattering into the saucer. 'It would be foolish to try. You'd be the first suspect after taking out a hefty insurance and then he's popped off. Well, you know what I mean.'

'Not if you were somewhere else and had a cast iron alibi,' Jane said. 'I mean if it looked like he died as a result of an accident.'

'I wouldn't mind if somebody else did it,' Anne popped in.

Jane gave a little flutter of her hands, indicating for the others to lean forward closer. The heads of all four moved closer to the centre of the table as she whispered, 'What if we got together and did it ourselves? Knock them off at different times, different places, and all that?'

Then they all leaned back and gave serious looks to each other, the silence around the table very deafening within the café's hubbub. Jane leaned forward again.

'Let's not say anymore on this now. What I suggest is that if we are interested, let's meet again in about a month's time, say at the wine bar next door for lunch, and then talk? Say about one o'clock?'

She looked at Penny who nodded straight away. Francis, after a slight hesitation, then at Anne, who flushed with the three pairs of eyes on her, and dropping her own eyes, slowly nodded, and so an agreed date and time was set.

'Well,' Penny said. 'As I live here in London, shall I book a table for then?'

'Good idea,' Jane replied.

'My God, is that the time!' Anne exclaimed. 'I've got to get home. He has to have his dinner on the table at exactly six fifteen.' As she grabbed at her handbag and carrier bag, Jane caught hold of her wrist.

'Think what it would be like if you didn't have to rush, ever again,' she whispered softly, slowly letting go. 'See you next month?'

'Maybe you will,' she replied, 'maybe I will see you all. Bye for now.' Then with a flurry of coat and bag, she left the table and made her way out of the café.

'I'd better make a move too,' said Jane, 'maybe I'll catch the bastard in bed with one of his tarts and do the job myself.'

'Without the insurance?' Penny asked.

'You're right! See you next month then, and, oh,' she gave a throaty chuckle, 'I forgot. There's a horse in the three forty five tomorrow. Put your shirt on it. It's hot at twenty to one.' She picked up her things and was just leaving the table.

'What's the name?' queried Francis.

"Blood Money," Jane laughed as she left.

'Well if that horse comes in I'll see it as an omen and be here next month,' Francis said, putting out her hand. Penny took it and said softly,

'See you next month.'

Ironically, the horse did win…

If you enjoyed this sample then look for **The Square Circle**.

Also by this Author:

[The Painted Sword](#)

[Cruise Control](#)

[Wild Pleasures](#)

[Lending My Beloved](#)

[Lady of Cuckolds](#)

[Lady of Pleasure](#)

[Lady Magenta](#)

[Sexually Overdosed](#)

[Meeting My Fancy Dear](#)

[Prison Sex Slave](#)

[Chasing A Shadow](#)

[The Hostel](#)

[The Island](#)

[Thirst for Drugs and Pleasure](#)

[Forgotten Identity](#)

[Grey Memories](#)

[Chronos: Time Machine](#)

[The Hard Bomber](#)

[Honeymoon Abduction](#)

[The Yacht Sins](#)

From the Author

WANT FREE COPIES OF MY BOOKS?
Just visit my blog and download free copies of my books:
amy-redek.awesomeauthors.org/amy-redek

Author Central – http://www.amazon.com/Amy-Redek/e/B00A48NQ72

If you enjoyed any of my books then please share the love and click like on my books in Amazon.

If you write me a review and send me an email I will send you a free book, or many.
(Just know that these emails are filtered by my publisher.)

Good news is always welcome.

One Last Thing, For Kindle Readers...

When you turn the page, Kindle will give you the opportunity to rate this book and share your thoughts on Facebook and Twitter. If you enjoyed my writings, would you please take a few seconds to let your friends know about it? Because... when they enjoy they will be grateful to you and so will I.

Thank You!

Amy Redek
amy_redek@awesomeauthors.org

About the Author

George Eliot was a famous writer, though at the time, only male authors were recognised. It was in fact the pen name of Mary Ann Evans, a female.

When I started writing, I thought that if a woman could use a male name, why, with me being male, why couldn't I use the name of a female? Though to be different, I made my writer's name from an anagram of my real name.

I wasn't the brightest spark in my school days and it was only while being in the Merchant Navy did I self-educate myself. That being mostly literature, classical music and artists, like Tolstoy, Chopin and Rembrandt. After leaving the navy, I had several jobs, finishing up by being a working boss using my own maxim that 'Management is the art of delegation.'

It's when I became self-employed that I began to write, though sadly, not many of my books can be published because of certain laws that forbid certain aspects of life. This never fazed me for I was really writing just to please myself having a wide range of the human psych.

Having written ninety stories, my only aim now is to reach one hundred. I give thanks to the publishers for at least putting some of my efforts out for others to enjoy as much as I did in the writing of them.

You may also like the books by these authors:

EVERYTHING
I Wanted To Do

BY
SCOUT ALLEN

"Did you ever think we'd be doing this?" she asked as she pulled off her shirt and unbuckled her pants.

"Yeah but not without getting arrested," I commented while I slipped off my pants and pulled off my shirt.

We were in the country of Italy, Rome more specifically, at the fountain of Trevi. You know that large fountain with statues of horses and Italian people, large water out front and sprayers?

Anyway, I and my friend had been doing the whole backpacking through Europe thing when the Disappearance happened.

"Hey what are you doing?" I asked as she was pulling down her panties.

"What? If I'm going to go swimming in Rome's world famous Trevi fountain, I'm going to do it naked," then she pulled off her bra and looked at me. "Aren't you?"

Samantha wasn't a curvy goddess but she was pretty. Five foot six, B-cup breasts, bright red hair, blue eyes just bright enough to catch the eye, slim but not starvingly so, with slight hips that go down to a strip of hair leading to her otherwise bare sex. She was the most beautiful woman I'd seen in ages.

"Julian?" she said as I checked her out, her not shy in the least.

"Oh yeah," and I quickly stripped out of my shorts.

Climbing over the stone edge, we began our swimming around, thankfully because my penis had become erect.

"I wonder where they all went," she mused for what seemed like the hundredth time.

"Who knows," I added.

Not three days ago, the world seemed to have enough of the people's bullshit and it seemed like everyone else was just...gone. No clothing left over, no corpses to clean up, no crashes of cars. Time seemed to stop for everyone. And then when it was back, we were alone.

Thinking to myself, I wondered where everyone was, what they were doing, how we were missed in it all.

Something touched my skin and I fumbled and partially drowned myself before coming up for air. Sam was laughing out loud and standing on her feet, her bare breasts jiggling as she laughed.

I was now painfully erect.

"Why you.." and I tackled her back into the water as we wrestled and splashed until we ended up against one statue with my back pressed against the wall and her pressed against me.

We were both panting from the exertion. Her bare skin pressed against mine, her breasts pressed against my chest as she looked into my eyes. My painfully erect penis pressed against her warm crotch. Something came to mind but I decided not to say it. Instead, I simply moved my hands down to her ass and gripped it.

We'd been alone together for three days, no sex for weeks for either of us. We were young, horny, and willing.

I kissed her and she kissed me back.

Pulling her ass so her lips where pressed against my cock, her soft skin in my hands as her hands roamed over my chest and skin sending ripples of pleasure through my body. She was hungry, lustful... so was I...

If you enjoyed this sample then look for <u>Everything I Wanted To Do</u>.

WHITE CRAVING *For* BLACK

HOT EROTICA

SAMMY WEST

"Hi honey, come on in" Her hand reached out and I climbed in hearing the door swish shut behind me.

Sherie shared the back with 1 other, an older black guy wearing a suit, I guessed in his mid to late fifties, he said nothing as I flopped on the seat opposite him, his face expressionless and his eyes covered with dark sunglasses.

"How are you? This is Steve" she gushed as her palm gestured towards our fellow passenger.

The van suddenly jerked into life tinted glass partition separated us from our driver,

"I'm very well thanks" my voice took on a kind of squeaky tone as I felt my throat begin to dry suddenly, wondering what on earth I had let myself in for.

"Are you nervous? Nah don't be silly, it is going to be a great day for us all." Her enthusiasm seemed catching as a smile spread across my face.

Steve turned to her and whispered something in her ear,

"Honey could you just lift that dress a little for us" she asked before turning back to Steve.

I eased my dress up a little, lifting my bum from the seat enough so I could move it above my pull-ups and he nodded appreciatively.

"Well that's test 1 completed." Her dark puffy lips parted into another of her beaming smiles, revealing perfect white teeth.

Steve whispered once again, his face still emotionless, his eyes a mystery behind those gold-rimmed sunglasses.

"Time for test 2 already babe" she fixed my gaze then her eyes wandered to his crotch. I watched as her hands undid him and suddenly began to feel sick, my stomach in a knot as the reality began to unfold.

I had known all along this was not going to be some innocent little drinks party, I knew that it was inevitably going to involve some romp but now I started to realize that I was going to have very little say in the forthcoming events. In fact I doubted my opinion would even matter at all, thoughts raced through my mind as I watched her pull out a very dark, thick but flaccid manhood. She looked across and smiled, her eyes narrowing slightly giving her an almost menacing look.

He reached across with a long cane and tapped the end between my legs silently commanding me to part them, my lace covered pussy now in full view.

"Let's see you play with that white organ" The playfulness now disappeared from Sherie's voice.

I felt my mouth suddenly dry up, I knew that anything but a positive answer was futile and began to reach down between my legs his face remaining expressionless as my finger pulled aside my knickers exposing my dampening self..

If you enjoyed this sample then look for **White Craving For Black**.

ANGUS
MacGREGOR

RESCUED

HOT ROMANCE EROTICA

THE PARDONED SERIES, BOOK 2

She giggled to herself remembering when she was younger, just really beginning to be curious about boys. One night when Jack had been complaining of allergies, she had intentionally given him way too much Benadryl which knocked him out. She waited until the house was dark and still, and sneaked into his room, pulled back the covers, and cautiously slid his underwear down. She stared at his penis, now large and man-sized, framed with soft brown curls, as it hardened in the cool air and soon lay back against his soft belly. She had no sexual attraction to Jack, but part of her wanted to hold his dick and just see what it felt like. She had the distinct feeling that he wouldn't have minded. She finally stretched out her hand and held the heavy shaft and marveled at how soft and hard it was at the same time stroking the shaft up and down until he was rock hard and a clear drop of pre-cum oozed from the tip. She had thrown the covers back over him and ran to her room, embarrassed and aroused at the same time. As she lie in the quiet of her own bed, she slid her hand down between her legs and rubbed her clit as images of Jack were replaced with Charlie Morris, a handsome boy from her Algebra II class. He sat beside her, and Cassie had noticed that he was constantly adjusting his dick in class. Often when he was asked to go to the whiteboard to work a problem, his erection pressed hard against his jeans revealing a thick round head. She imaged her hand sliding up and down his hard cock, lowering her head to his lap, feeling the heat of his member in her hand and against her face as she brought herself to a shattering climax.

Cassie grinned thinking how much Jack would love that story and would give her hell for being such a perv. He would offer to show her the real thing again any time she wanted, she figured. Her little sister Carly was sweet but interestingly, Cassie didn't feel nearly as close to her. The two of them had hardly ever spoken about boys and sex, whereas she and Jack were always bouncing their exploits off each other. Of course in her case, they were so few she didn't bother saying too much. Jack, on the other hand, enjoyed being as shockingly graphic with her as he could be, but a big part of her enjoyed the playful, dirty talk.

Cassie had a few close calls in high school. The most intense was with Charlie Morris, who had asked her to prom when she was a junior. The two had spent a few fun hours on her bed or his when their families weren't around. The week before prom, he had pulled his dick out, and she finally got to really touch it. He pushed his jeans and shorts down to his ankles and pulled his shirt up to his neck. She knew he wanted her to suck it, but she wasn't sure about that. As she stroked his penis, he softly stroked the lips of her vagina and teased with the opening, which was wet and wanting. She gasped as his finger slid gently inside her as they kissed. Her hand sped up stroking his cock until he groaned. She watched as thick pearly ropes of semen blasted on his firm belly and got caught in the soft light brown hairs that ran from his navel to his groin.

After prom, the two had driven to a logging landing out on Baber Mountain. The night had been warm for May. Cassie had smiled when she saw the planning Charlie had done to for the night. He made a comfy place on the back of his pickup bed. The two sipped some lemon-flavored vodka, which was horrible, and lay with their formal clothes while they kissed and groped each other.

Cassie remembered his penis straining against the thin fabric of the tuxedo pants…

If you enjoyed this sample then look for **Rescued**.

Nicki Homewood

The Debtor's Performance

Exhibitionist Erotica

I sat at the table and prayed for a number higher than eight. The dice felt warm in my sweaty hand and I could feel my heart pounding in my chest. They rolled round inside my hand and I scattered them down the table, closing my eyes at the final moment of ejection as they made their way down the table and settled.

I let my head fall backwards, tried to relax my neck, feeling my rich golden hair fall down my back, hoping against hope that finally my luck had changed. I heard the girl next to me gasp and I tried to determine what that meant for me. Had I won at last?

Three and Two.

Not enough, not nearly enough.

What would happen next, I wondered. I was so far beyond the limit of credit that I had initially agreed that I could not believe they would let me borrow more. My credit cards were already maxed out and however good a customer I was, I couldn't believe that they would let me keep on playing. I had already had an interview with Mr Abadlioi last week after the previous set of losses.

I looked down at the beautiful blue satin dress that I was wearing. I had picked it out because the last time I had worn it, I had been lucky, had come away better than level. I loved the big slit down the front, the way that it showed off so much of my cleavage. Around the casino there were certain rules of behaviour that I loved. Guys could admire a beautiful woman and women could be admired, but no one would make much of a move, no one would hassle you. It was nice, and safe.

Economically it was not safe, I reflected. Economically it was a disaster, a life-changing, misery-inducing, marriage-destroying disaster.

I could feel my string pulling into my ass a little, the tops of my stockings on my hips, the lace gently hugging me to keep themselves in place. The satin was smooth and sexy against my skin and I thought that I may never be able to afford to buy such a garment again.

Silence descended over the table as behind me I could hear a group of people approaching me. I turned slowly with a forced smile on my lips.

"Mrs DiAngelo, perhaps I could suggest that you come this way," Mr Abadlioi asked, a cold politeness still evident in his voice.

Behind him were two guys, not goons exactly but big guys that could look after themselves in a fight I was sure. Not that fighting was exactly my thing.

We walked away from the table and I could feel the eyes of all the people on the floor track me as I walked out past the tables, past the fruit machines and down a darker corridor leading to the backrooms where the reality of casino debts started to encroach on real life. No longer here were you just dealing in coloured plastic chips, this was where cheques and credit cards lived, and debt collectors and lawyers I supposed.

The guys on either side of me didn't even look at me. Here I was wearing a practically skin tight satin dress, pulled tight over my tits, accentuating my 34B breasts that were otherwise unencumbered with cover or support. I knew that men found this dress very sexy. I had seen the looks of lust, of desire in their eyes many times. I knew that my husband loved to see me in it, loved to see the way it showed the lines of my firm breasts, and just gave away a little of my nipples as they pressed into the fabric.

I was shown once again into his office and sat down opposite him, ensconced behind his huge solid oak desk. He smiled at me graciously.

"Well, Mrs DiAngelo, we seem to find ourselves here again. Well, well, well. And so soon," he started.

"I seem to be going through a very unlucky run," I mumbled nervously.

"Yes, well that is certainly clear. But the problem for me is now really just how we are going to recover the funds. I seem to remember last time that you were very keen to keep it between the two of us. Does that remain the case?" he asked, his eyes roaming down over my form.

If you enjoyed this sample then look for **The Debtor's Performance**.

THREESOMES EROTICA
DOUG AND DIANE SERIES, BOOK 1

AND MASSEUSE
Makes Three

IAN MACSWAIN

I am a professional masseuse, and have been for many years. When I say professional, I mean that I do massage strictly with no funny business, or hanky panky. My husband is a successful businessman, so I don't have to work as hard as some of my other LMT friends, but I take my work very seriously. My kids are old enough so that my not being at home when they get home from school is not an issue anymore either. This allows me the freedom to set a pretty flexible schedule.

I have a pair of clients, a husband and wife couple, that I have been massaging for quite a number of years. Doug and Diane are a very active couple with two kids in junior high school. Doug designs websites and Diane owns a floral shop. They do very nicely. Their house is up in the hills on about 10 acres of land, with a spectacular view. We have gotten very friendly over the years, like old friends. When I go to massage them, we usually sit and talk for a while and have a glass of wine on the deck. They are such regular clients that I leave one of my massage tables at their house; they dedicated a room to it. Our relationship has always been totally professional.

Until recently.

A couple of weeks ago, I got a call from Doug, on the morning of one of our appointments, asking if he could meet me for lunch. This was a bit of an irregular request but we had become close enough client/friends that I agreed and we met at a nice restaurant near his office. We chatted for a while, about family stuff, some business chit chat until he got around to the point and mentioned their upcoming 17th anniversary; coming up the following weekend. They had both agreed that they wanted to do something really special. Doug seemed very nervous. I asked him what was wrong.

"This is really tough to say," he stammered. "And I don't want to make you feel weird." He paused a while before continuing. "Diane and I both really enjoy your company. We think of you as a good friend, as well as our health professional." I told him that I considered them more than simply clients. "Well, we wanted to,...well, ask you if..." He trailed off again.

"I'm not following." I told him.

"We really don't want to risk our friendship with you." He said slowly. "We wanted to know if...you would consider...getting closer."

"Closer?" I asked, unsure what he meant.

"Well, at the risk of offending you, ..." He was starting to hem and haw about our earlier discussion about professionalism with my work, keeping it totally professional. "We were wondering if you would consider indulging us in a more,... sensual,... kind of massage."

"More sensual?" I asked. "You mean sexual?"

"No, no." He stumbled. "Well, unless..." There was a long look between us, wherein I said nothing.

"This is not going, ... you know, forget it. I'm sorry if, ..." We shared a long fairly awkward silence. I think I know what he was saying, and with any other person, I would be up and out of there already. I knew these people, though. This was not something that would drive me out of my chair as I thought it might. I really liked them and Doug was really embarrassed now.

"Hey. It's okay." I told him, trying to prevent him having the heart attack he appeared to be having. I admit that I was intrigued as to what they might be considering, as a couple. It was their anniversary after all. "Just tell me what's on your mind."

"Diane was in a panic over being the one to ask, but now I wish she was here, ..." I simply waited, trying not to look as flustered as I felt. I had only had to deal with these kinds of come-ons a couple of times, and had simply packed my shit and walked out; perhaps a bit stern a response but I wasn't having this discussion with strangers, men.

"Diane and I both really like you. We both think that you're awesome at what you do. And ... honestly ... we both find you very attractive, and we have both been considering ... you know ... a ... something different." Doug's hands were fluttering as if trying to not say something too outlandish. "Not that you ...", he stammered. I smiled at him.

"When I started in this line of work, I swore that I would never get involved in anything sexual with my clients." He looked a bit sad and ashamed for asking. "Don't get me wrong, I'm very flattered that you are asking. I think that you are both very attractive. Very! I suppose if I was ever to consider something like that, it would probably be with people like you two."

"But, ..." he trailed off. "I hope that you're not offended."

"No. Truly."

"I'm sorry. I really am. I hate to make you feel uncomfortable." I assured him that it was fine; that I wasn't, though secretly I was. My mind was suddenly filled with thoughts of what they might be thinking. I caught myself flashing on both their bodies. I had been their massage therapist for a while and had seen most of them already. Diane's bottom flashed into my mind, unbidden. I had to shake my head to clear it. "Will you still make our appointment tonight?"

I patted his hand. "Of course. Believe me. It's okay." He remained uncomfortable through the rest of lunch and seemed ready as hell to get out of there. The conversation was perfunctory at best; the kids' schooling, the weather; it was agony. I tried to think of something to ease his mind. I didn't want them to be embarrassed for their appointments tonight. He shook my hand rather mechanically when we stepped out onto the street, and he walked away rather briskly. I felt so bad for him. Why I didn't feel worse for myself, I don't know.

I didn't mention my lunch to my husband when I got home, as there wasn't enough time to really get into it. The kids needed feeding and then homework had to be done. I left them in front of the TV as I headed out. Later that evening when I got to their house, I felt like Diane in particular was really embarrassed. It remained that way until we were alone and I was massaging her.

I worked on her in silence until I asked, "Are you okay?"

"Yeah, I'm fine. Why?"

"You seem so quiet."

"Oh, I'm sorry. It's just that … well, I'm a little embarrassed." I asked her about what.

"Well, having Doug ask you to help us with our little … fantasy."

"Oh, please. Don't be embarrassed. Besides, we didn't really get into that much detail."

"I'm sorry for putting you on the spot like that."

"Please don't be." I told her quietly. "Besides, I'm flattered." There was a very long silence for a while, then I asked her, "I was just caught a bit… off guard." She apologized again. I just… keep my business, well… like a business." She said that she totally understood and that she hoped I wouldn't think them weird or anything. "Oh, not at all. What people do behind closed doors…" I was sounding like I was discussing it like I knew their private life. I dropped it.

There was a very long period of silence, while I continued her shoulders and back. "I just don't want you to have the wrong idea about us." She said finally.

"I don't have any idea… It's between you guys."

"It's just a stupid fantasy kind of thing." I didn't ask what. "Perhaps they are better as fantasies anyway." She said at last. I hummed that maybe so. I finished her legs and then held the sheet for her as she rolled over.

"What is your fantasy?" I suddenly blurted, not meaning to. We remained silent for a while. She then quietly and haltingly told me how they had discussed getting a sensual massage. She was nervous about the details, so I continued to press her gently. She described a scene with soft sexy music, dim lights and lots of candles, and a sexy scene wherein a female masseuse would be topless or nude, and there would be a lot of intimate touching, between all of them. I admitted to myself that it sounded kind of cool and that my husband Josh would probably love such a thing.

She continued that Doug would help massage Diane and then vice versa. She even admitted to being curious about being with another woman. She must have talked for half an hour about what she would like to try and watch her husband try. I told her that that sounded like a magical anniversary. She admitted that maybe they should keep it as just a fantasy. I asked her if they did want to fulfill this fantasy what they would do about making it happen. She thought they might call an escort service. We left it at that.

Throughout the rest of her massage and Doug's, I kept thinking about them and the way they looked nude. Doug was silent the entire time. I was becoming intrigued with the idea of them wanting to try something new and erotic; do it together and share the experience. Even after I left their house, I couldn't get it out of my head. When I got home, the kids were asleep and Josh was reading in bed. I mentioned it to my husband, who was already half-asleep. He told me that it sounded like fun to him, and that I might enjoy it. He rolled over and turned out the light, but that comment kept me up half the night. It sounded like fun to him. And what did he mean I might enjoy it?

If you enjoyed this sample then look for **And Masseuse Makes Three.**

WANT FREE COPIES OF MY BOOKS?
Just visit my blog and download free copies of my books:
amy-redek.awesomeauthors.org/amy-redek

www.ingramcontent.com/pod-product-compliance
Lightning Source LLC
Chambersburg PA
CBHW071346170626
46811CB00003B/1003